MOUSE OF ILL REPUTE

ELLEN RIGGS

BOUGHT-THE-FARM
MYSTERIES

FREE PREQUEL

Rescuing this pup could bring Ivy a whole new life... if it doesn't kill her first.

Discover how big city executive Ivy meets Keats, her crime-solving sheepdog, in A Dog with Two Tales. Ivy Galloway doesn't know how desperate she is to escape the big city and her soul-sucking corporate career until she meets a sheepdog in need of rescue, too.

This short prequel to the laugh-out-loud Bought-the-Farm Mystery series is a page-turner for lovers of animals, humor and spunky amateur sleuths. Go to **ellenriggs.com/opt-in** and join Ellen Riggs' author newsletter to get this FREE prequel.

Mouse of Ill Repute

Copyright © 2023 Ellen Riggs

ISBN 978-1-998742-12-7 D2D Paperback
ISBN 978-1-990613-50-0 eBook
ISBN 978-1-990613-49-4 Book
ISBN 978-1-990613-51-7 AudioBook
ASIN B0CL8PQXHG. Kindle
ASIN. 1990613497. Paperback

Publisher: Ellen Riggs
www.ellenriggs.com
Cover designer: Lou Harper
Editor: Serena Clarke
2512230222D2D

CHAPTER ONE

I walked out of the barn and onto the gravel driveway, musing over the skirmish between two of my favorite goats. Lucy and Ethel were sisters but had never been friends. Today, something set them off, and Charlie, my farm manager, had put up a temporary fence within the pasture leaving a goat clique on either side. Since the sisters were in good health, I would need to dig deeper to get to the bottom of the animosity. Charlie told me not to worry about it and reminded me that the livestock at Runaway Farm weren't a corporate team like the one I led for years as a human resources executive. Maybe not, but was it wrong to want my goats to get along? To graze in peace and harmony? To reach their full caprine potential?

Keats, my canine sidekick, gave a mumble beside me. A "goats will be goats" kind of sound. He had little patience with the moods of rescue livestock. Ethel received a sharp nip to tell her so, whereas Lucy got chased to the corner of the pasture to cool her heels.

If goats had heels. I should probably know that by now, but it was a gap in knowledge that a few taps on my phone could remedy. Reaching into my pocket, I spoke over Keats' next rumble. "Yeah, I know we need to get on the road to beat the Friday rush. This will only take a sec."

His protest escalated. It had a "don't say I didn't warn you" quality that made me give up on the phone.

"What's going on, buddy?" Nothing looked suspicious to me. Jilly Blackwood, my best friend, was coming down the front stairs with a small suitcase in one hand and a cat carrier in the other. We were going away and I wasn't thrilled about leaving a livestock problem behind. I firmly believed no one could settle a goat dispute better than someone with a decade's experience in corporate mediation. "I don't see anything amiss."

The dog nudged my leg, perhaps to suggest using my other senses. When my ears and nose failed me, too, he took pity on his flawed human and dropped to a crouch. With his belly brushing gravel, he moved forward in slow motion. Orange, yellow and red maple leaves didn't so much as crackle under his paws.

Someone—or something—was hiding behind the truck, out of my sight and Jilly's.

I began following but one crunch of my work boot earned me a scornful glare from the dog's eerie blue eye. His brown eye was kinder, but the message was clear: leave this to me.

Signaling Jilly to stay where she was, I bent over to peer between the vehicle's wheels. What I saw made me grin.

Keats' rear came up and then he lunged around the truck. In the same instant, two voices shouted, "Boo!"

A screech followed, accompanied by an "Ow!"

The other person bellowed, "Dagnabit! Stop, you cur."

"Happy Halloween," I called. "Come out, come out whoever you are."

Two heads popped up over the bed of the pickup. One woman was wearing a leather cowboy hat, the other an army helmet. They came toward me jerking and hopping, as my herding department meted out motivation. Neither had a good word to say about him.

A stranger might well have assumed the two octogenarians were in costume. Gertie Rhodes was wearing a ratty brown poncho over the unmistakable shape of a rifle, while Edna Evans was in full army camouflage. They weren't dressed for Halloween, however. This was just another day in paradise for them.

"Call him off," Edna said. "Can't your dog take a joke, Ivy Galloway?"

Keats looked up at me, his mouth hanging open in a pant-laugh.

"I've rarely seen him more amused," I said. "But the joke's on you. Never prank a gal with a sheepdog."

By the time they'd joined me, Jilly had reached us, too. She set the cat carrier down and shook her finger at the older women. "Don't you have better things to do than scare Ivy?"

The old friends looked at each other and then cackled in unison. "Not really," Edna said. "It's Halloween. Isn't that what you're supposed to do? Scare people?"

Opening the back door of the truck, Jilly slid the cat carrier into the middle and snapped the seatbelt through the handle. Percy let out a soulful wail. He preferred to be loose, but on longer trips, we generally secured him. "Halloween is stupid," she said. "And you have more important things to do than rattle the nerves of someone with PTSD and a half-healed concussion."

My best friend had golden curls, sparkling green eyes and a sharp coat, but she was as fierce a warrior as the seniors. Jilly just executed her battles with the style, grace and tenacity of a former corporate shark.

I smiled to let her know I was fine. "They tried, they lost. It's possible to ambush an absent-minded hobby farmer, but not her savvy dog."

Keats gave Edna's jumpsuit a last nip and judging by her leap, his teeth hit skin.

Sweeping her hand toward the truck like a gameshow host, Jilly said, "Let's deploy."

Edna went around to climb in on the passenger side. "Why so sour, Jillian? Someone steal your candy apple?"

I opened my door and let Keats jump through to land on Jilly's lap. He gave her cheek a slurp and she clutched him with both hands. "I hate Halloween and when it falls on a Saturday, so much the worse."

"We're heading to a Halloween party," Gertie pointed out. "Put on your happy mask."

"It's not a party," I said, turning the key in the ignition. "It's a pet rescue event."

"With a Halloween theme." Gertie stuck a flyer through the seats. "And a costume party."

We'd seen the flyer, and even distributed copies around Clover Grove. Our friends from the Dorset Hills pet Rescue Mafia had organized the weekend event in Thistledown and enlisted our help. Their annual Thanksgiving Rescue Pageant would take place in a few weeks, but this year there were so many worthy dogs in need of homes they'd decided to expand to new territory.

My homesteading town was nearly maxed out on pets, but Thistledown held promise. It was an up-and-comer among satellite communities for Dorset Hills, the shining star of Hill Country. We all benefited from the attention and tourist dollars "Dog Town" attracted and we were always happy to support our friends in rescue. They did good work, not all of it legal. I respected that, too, despite being engaged to an officer of the law.

"I didn't see Cori as the Halloween type," Jilly said, her fingers still flying over Keats. It was Percy's orange fluff she needed right now. Keats was normally willing to pinch hit, but his paws moved to the dashboard to embrace adventure. "It's not a real holiday."

"Tell that to the local kids," Gertie said. "What's the harm in dressing up and collecting candy? Didn't you do it?"

I let the truck roll slowly down the long lane, taking in the brilliant colors on either side. The leaves never lasted long enough and many trees had already shed their fall finery.

Jilly didn't answer as we coasted under the iron sign that arched over the lane. It said "Runaway Far" because the "m" had rusted out. I left it like that because I'd run away far from my unhappy life in the city and wanted our guests at the inn to enjoy the same sense of escape. I didn't like running anymore. My place was here, among my animals, especially when they were bickering.

"No, I didn't," Jilly said, at last. "My mom wouldn't let me. People said she was a witch, remember." Keats turned to give her a blast of warmth from his brown eye. "She *was* a witch, but not in the way they thought."

I laughed. "Is that why you don't talk about her much?"

She held up both hands. "Not enough fingers to count the ways."

"And then there's your mother-in-law, my friend. She's no sack of candy either."

Jilly finally mustered a small smile. "Dahlia may be flighty, but no one suggests there's a broomstick involved."

A thump from behind made golden curls bounce off the headrest. "Jillian, take a moment and be grateful."

My best friend turned and scowled at Edna. "Grateful that people thought my mom was a witch?"

"Grateful that people weren't calling *you* the witch. It's been said of me often enough."

Edna wasn't wrong. I'd said so myself when I moved home. Little did I know Edna would save my life and become one of my best friends. Her steed of choice wasn't a broom, but an ATV.

"Oh, they did," Jilly said. "The entire family got the label."

Gertie cackled again. "Me, too. Back when I was shooting trespassers' soles." She paused for a moment. "That sounded odd, but I meant their shoes."

"Sounded right for Halloween." I turned into the parking lot at Mandy's Country Store. "And I guess that makes us all witches, because people say it about me, too."

Jilly turned indignantly. "Who says that?"

"Lots of people. They hear me talking to Keats and Percy and figure I'm either nuts or oozing black magic."

"That's ridiculous. Everyone talks to their pets." She reached back and touched Percy's crate. "Don't they, cat-baby?"

There were smiles all around as we got out of the truck, but our cheer faded by the time we got inside. Mandy, our friend and baker extraordinaire, had decked out the store in full Halloween glory, from displays of straw bales and pumpkins to a giant hairy spider on one of the stools.

Coming around the counter, she grinned at me. "Not on your favorite stool, Ivy. And it can be relocated if you folks want to sit down."

"Oh, Mandy," Jilly said. "You know Halloween isn't a real holiday. It's totally bogus."

The storekeeper crossed thin arms over her chest as if to ward off attack. Mandy had been painfully shy until a murder two years ago shook her voice loose. She used it now. "All holidays are real in retail, including Halloween. It's taken over from Valentine's and all the other bogus retail holidays." Gesturing to a glass case, she added, "Have you tried my tarantula treats?"

I eyed the brown blobs that featured eight chocolate-dipped legs and bulging candy eyeballs. "Gimme half a dozen of those. Plus some iced sugar cookies. A ghost, a ghoul and four witches, please."

"To stay or go?"

It said a lot that Mandy thought I could tackle them all on my favorite stool. On a different day, I might. "To go. Plus a pumpkin spice latte. That's something new here, but I smell it."

She nodded before heading back to the counter. "Another retail compromise. Turns out pumpkin spice lattes are a season unto themselves."

"Just a black coffee for me," Edna said. "There won't be such nonsense after the end times. Ghouls on cookies? Lunacy."

"By then you'll have real ghouls, and zombies, too," I said. "Good thing you're already a witch." Turning, I shouted at Mandy over the screaming milk frother. "Tell them people call me a witch, Mandy."

Her blue eyes widened as she peered over her shoulder. "I will not."

Jilly gave me a light shove. "Stop it, Ivy. Mandy deserves better."

"I do." Mandy poured milk with a light hand into my takeaway cup and then sprinkled it with cinnamon. "And I've been called worse than a witch. A murderer."

I accepted the hot beverage. "That's terrible, and a lie." Mandy had once withheld information that nearly got me killed, but she couldn't have known. What's more, she had made up for her omission countless times. I gave her a contrite smile now. "We're heading to Thistledown for the pet rescue competition."

Mandy moved on to boxing my treats. "Competition? I heard shelters are bursting at the seams. Aren't there enough to go around without making people jump through hoops?"

"Not like these," Jilly said. "The Rescue Mafia trains the best of the best and matches people with their perfect dog. There are only a few available and people need to run the gauntlet to win one."

"Anyone would be lucky to get a Mafia rescue," I said. "They take most of the work and risk out of dog ownership."

Keats gave an annoyed grumble, perhaps suggesting that the work and risk were what made the enterprise worthwhile. I smiled down at him. Rescuing him had been the most terrifying moment of my life—one that made Halloween look utterly vapid—but I had been lucky as far as training was concerned. We'd joined classes because I wanted to follow the standard rules of puppy ownership but Keats had pretty much trained himself. When he cared to be a model dog, he played the role well, but much of the time I let him use his own instincts and judgement. To me, that was sound dog rearing.

Mandy handed me the box and then offered a plate of the decorated sugar cookies to my friends. For all her protests, Edna was quick to nab a cheery ghoul, while Gertie went with the classic bat. Jilly selected a grinning jack-o'-lantern, whereas I deliberated before choosing a cute little mouse with long whiskers. At least, I hoped it was a mouse, and not its more robust relative.

I was about to take a bite when Mandy said, "You'll check in with Thelma Tilrow at the schoolhouse library, right?"

"Of course. It's the central location for the event. Why?"

If I'd been alone Mandy would have spilled what she knew, but she hesitated in front of Edna and Gertie. "Dottie Bridges was in this week telling me tales about Halloween in Thistledown. Stories she heard from Thelma."

The two librarians were best friends and part of my inner circle, despite a rough start with Dottie. I had learned to keep an open mind because enemies didn't always stay that way.

Edna's mouth opened to press Mandy for information, but I motioned to Keats to start herding. "Let's leave a little mystery for when we get there."

The dog wasted no time in driving the others out the door, letting me lag to thank Mandy. She was my first stop when I had a case, even when I didn't know there *was* a case.

"It's probably just one of those urban myths," she said, as I walked out. "Or in this case, a rural myth. But be careful, Ivy."

"I'm always careful." We shared a good laugh at that blatant lie as I started down the stairs to join Jilly. "Save me some tarantulas, okay? Never thought I'd have cause to say that."

My best friend rolled her eyes. "I cannot wait till Halloween is over. As if life weren't hard enough without glamorizing horror."

I linked my arm through hers as we headed to the truck. "It's just as well we'll be away from home on the big night, my friend."

"Why? We don't get trick-or-treaters anyway. Even if we lived closer to town, most parents would refuse to bring their kids to the farm at night."

"Just because we've had legit murders? I'll bet the true crime trend hits Clover Grove, soon, too."

She gave a disgusted snort. "I don't understand that at all. Who wants to be scared?"

Keats panted a quick ha-ha-ha and I laughed, too. "Us? I mean, we do go out of our way to walk toward crime rather than away from it."

"That's different. We're not treating it like entertainment. We're trying to do something about it."

"Definitely not entertainment," I agreed. "By the way, your husband was the one who ruined Halloween for me when we were kids. He loved jumping out of closets wearing fright masks. Mom punished her golden boy by holding him back from trick-or-treating one year, which only punished me because Asher claimed all my candy as his. I did the work, he reaped the spoils."

Jilly laughed. "It's a wonder you two grew up to be so... I was going to say normal, but does the word really apply?"

I opened the truck door for her. "Nope, but our past shaped us to be who we are."

"For better or worse. But if my husband tries that mask stunt on me he'll regret it."

"That's more like it, Jillian," Edna said, after I got behind the wheel. "It's time you stepped fully into your power."

Jilly balanced Keats on her legs as I pulled out and started rolling in the direction of Thistledown. "Thank goodness we can count on the library to be a safe zone. I don't think I can handle more horror."

She underestimated herself. Jilly could always handle what life threw at her.

Even when it was a body.

CHAPTER TWO

A s I pulled into the parking spot closest to the red schoolhouse library, something swung out of a tall maple tree, dangled directly in front of the windshield and then thumped heavily onto the hood.

Not something.

Someone.

We all screamed, and even in my panic, it struck me I hadn't heard a genuine note of terror in Edna's voice before. It transformed instantly to a war cry, however. That's what set us apart. I transitioned to battle when needed but never that fast. Speeding up my reaction time would save me a world of pain.

I clutched the steering wheel tight as the truck stuttered to a stall. The body now face down on the hood wore a green-and-black lumberjacket, black jeans, gloves and work boots. A balaclava covered his face. I could only guess it was a man from his size and the magnitude of the impact.

Two heads tried to push through the gap between the seats. "Dagnabit, Gertie, back off. I'm heading this army."

"I'm the one with the gun," Gertie said.

There was a scuffle and Edna growled, "Think you're the only one?"

I held up my hand. "Quiet. There's something strange here."

Jilly reached for my sleeve. "Ya think? There's a body on the hood, Ivy."

My eyes turned from the body to Keats. His ruff and tail were down, and his ears pricked and forward. I'd seen my dog in many a threatening situation and this didn't rank very high. "I think—"

Before I could finish, the body spasmed, flopping wildly on the hood. Its head came to rest right in front of me on the windshield and I leaned so far back in my seat the leather was in peril of cracking. The eyes in the holes of the balaclava peered in opposite directions.

The pant-laugh from Jilly's lap triggered a volley of inappropriate language from the back seat.

"My friends," I said, opening the door. "We've been pranked."

The body came to life once more, and I finally saw the fishing line. Someone stepped out from behind the big trunk of the maple and waved. She was wearing black knit gloves with orange middle fingers.

Cori Hogan reeled her faux corpse back up into the tree and then circled the trunk to tie it off. "That was awesome! Edna, I knew you could sing but you sure hit the high notes today."

The back doors of the truck opened and Cori flew up the ramp to the library door with Edna in pursuit. The older woman could move well, even in heavy boots, but the tiny dog trainer was fleet of foot and easily evaded her.

"I hope Edna leaves her to me," Jilly said, releasing Percy from his carrier. "This was everything I hate about Halloween wrapped up in an orange and black bow."

Keats waited for us on the ramp, panting happily. He adored Cori, and if I should ever be... well, permanently incapacitated... I suspected he'd shift his allegiance to her and work alongside Clem, her prizewinning border collie.

His dog smile vanished, as if my thought had appeared in a bubble over my head. Then he came back to collect me, giving my calf a nip of punishment for such disloyalty. He wasn't going anywhere, the nip said. Pranks were fun but they weren't the real work a sheepdog was born to do. He was happy with his life and Halloween was just an amiable diversion when there were no bickering livestock to corral or mysteries to solve.

After that, he ignored the decorations, of which there were many. Thelma had gone all out, with rope cobwebs, a plastic skeleton rattling over the door, a sheeted ghost dangling from the eaves, and cardboard cutouts of bats, witches, vampires and other creatures of the night.

Jilly continued a murmur of disgust but Percy climbed onto the railing to swat at drifting clouds of cotton fog. He was more like a dog than most dogs I'd known, but sometimes his feline genes triumphed.

Inside, there was no sign of either Cori or Edna. They were probably in the large back room that would serve as headquarters for the event. Gertie went on ahead to find them.

Thelma Tilrow, Thistledown's librarian, perched on a rolling stool behind her checkout desk wearing a long black cape. A plastic wand that pulsated through the light spectrum lay in front of her among neat stacks of index cards. Thelma was old school with her catalogue, yet modern enough to surf the dark web. She was one of many senior friends who defied all expectations for their vintage. Like Edna and Gertie, she seemed to age in reverse, getting a little younger and fitter each time I saw her. I attributed that to their involvement in solving crimes in our region. Instead of being sidelined, they were valued for their knowledge, even—albeit reluctantly —by the police.

One thing that never changed much among the older women,

however, was their hair. Gertie had the same braid as always, just a little longer. Edna regularly maintained her color and perm. And Thelma relied on hot rollers to secure her gray hair in sausages that resisted all but gale force winds. I would be surprised if the steepled witch hat sitting on the book cart behind her even fit on her head.

Thelma pushed away from her desk and rose without using her cane. "It's about time you got here. That Cori Hogan is a handful."

"No argument there," I said. "What's with all the Halloween hoopla? I didn't think you'd go in for this stuff. Dottie never does."

She arranged her robes over a prim tweed suit. "I never did before, either. But I've seen things this year that would... well, never mind. What really matters is that the community loves Halloween. There's enough sadness and hardship in the world. If cobwebs and plastic spiders bring a smile, I'm pleased to deliver." She swept the cape over one shoulder rather rakishly. "This rescue event will bring a lot of people to the library, and I want them to remember it. Let's get to work. You were tardy."

"Cool your curls, Thelma," Edna said, coming out of the back with Cori and Gertie. "The Mafia have put on a rescue show so many times they can do it in their sleep."

Thelma shushed her and pointed to a pair of women standing awkwardly at the end of the romantic poets' aisle. I knew that terrain well and had experienced mishaps there that didn't involve poetry, let alone romance.

Clapping gloved hands, Cori said, "Redding twins. Chop-chop. I expect my volunteers to show some hustle."

The spokes-Redding stepped forward. She had long caramel-colored hair, tasteful makeup, nice jeans, a leather jacket and matching boots. "We're not twins. And you haven't assigned us any tasks, yet."

The backup Redding joined her. They looked alike but not enough to be twins. I knew from my own sisters that Mother Nature often hit "repeat" when she found a design she liked. The five

Galloway Girls were often mistaken for one another despite a nearly 10-inch span in height. Our hair and eye coloring were similar, thanks to Mom's dominant genes. It would be easier with this pair because of their style differences. The backup Redding was wearing an orange sweater, very likely knit by hand, with an intricate pattern of bats and black cats. Although her hair color was similar to her sister's, there were no highlights, and it was tied in a ponytail. Her jeans and sneakers had seen better days. Or maybe not.

Cori shook her index finger, allowing a sliver of orange to show. "Back talk won't win you one of our dogs, Olivia. Or are you Kestle?"

"I'm Olive, and my sister is Kestra," the spokes-Redding said. "We're here to work, Ms. Hogan."

"Hard work won't win you one of our dogs, either." Cori's smile was more of a smirk. "But if you're lucky, it'll win you more work. We like worker bees."

Olive Redding hugged her fine leather bag. "What *will* win us one of your dogs, then?"

Summoning the sisters with a flourish of fingertips, Cori said, "The process can't be fully explained. We assess character based on performance during experiential tasks... with a bit of magic thrown in."

"Magic?" Kestra looked intrigued. "Is that woman really a—?" She pointed from Thelma to the steepled hat on the cart.

"Yes," Edna said.

"No," Jilly and I chorused.

"It's a compliment," Gertie said.

Thelma offered a stiff, standard-issue librarian smile. "Many would say I am a witch, and I take no issue with that."

A tall woman with blonde hair in an unruly topknot came down the hall with an elegant black setter at her side. Bridget Linsmore was the other half of the Rescue Mafia executive—the quieter, nicer half. She wasn't likely to explain to the Reddings that despite the performance element of the rescue events, decisions about placement really fell to Beau, her dog. He had uncanny intuition about character and the return rate on adopted dogs was negligible.

"All you need to do is be yourselves," Bridget said. "We appreciate your help to set up but once the event starts, just enjoy it."

"I don't enjoy competing," Olive said. "Isn't it enough that I'd love a dog and give it a good home?"

Cori and Bridget exchanged a look and the former laughed. "No. Anyone can love a dog, but few can be a good leader."

"I don't mind competing," Kestra said. "We've heard about your miraculous matches and I want one. There's so much risk in finding the right dog."

Cori gestured to each sister with more orange than necessary. "I get a strange vibe off you two. Is there trouble in sibling heaven?"

"Cori," I said. "It doesn't matter how well they get along unless they live together."

"We don't." Kestra's response was so hasty I knew Cori had hit the mark. These two were like my goats, Lucy and Ethel. "Never have."

Olive pulled on her sister's orange sleeve. "But we get along well enough, considering."

Cori stared at the orange sweater, sizing up the weaker link. "Considering what?"

"Kess, let me explain," Olive said. "I'm daughter number six, Kestra is number seven and we have a younger brother. That should give you an idea of our upbringing."

"Seriously?" Cori shook her head. "There's a limit of four dogs per household in most hill country municipalities. I don't see that children should be any different."

Kestra cut her eyes at her sister. "Maybe that's why they gave me away. To bring down the numbers."

"No one gave you away, Kess. Gran took you because you needed more attention than Mom had at the time. You grew up with the run of Howler Hall. That's hardly torture."

"Howler Hall?" I asked. "You mean the student center at Barkley College? I took summer courses there in high school."

"Figures," Cori said. "Keener."

"That's the place," Kestra said. "The state withdrew funding as enrolment dwindled. It's an all-ages community center now, with a focus on seniors."

"Our grandmother planned for Kess to take over as administrator," Olive added. "But my sister has a mind of her own."

"We like people with minds of their own," Cori said. "Although you two come with a lot of baggage. That's not going to win you a dog, either."

Keats circled in front of me and sat on my feet. "I've got baggage. And I found the perfect dog."

"'Found' being the operative word, Ivy. We wouldn't have given you one of ours." Cori was grinning, but Keats didn't like her tone. He took a little lunge at her, which she easily dodged. As the owner of a border collie, she was used to such moves.

I smiled at Kestra. "Don't worry too much. The right dog arrives at the right time. If it doesn't happen for you this weekend, don't take it to heart."

"There are only three dogs available, max," Bridget said. "Ten competitors have registered, so far."

"And we reserve the right to hold dogs back if we're not impressed," Cori said. "We're hard to impress."

The sisters' brows furrowed, making them look even more alike. "Can you tell us the events?" Olive asked.

"Typical Halloween stuff," Cori said. "I personally think it's silly but we're all about showmanship when it comes to fundraising for our dogs and I'll play to the theme." She turned to me. "Tell them, Ivy."

I rolled my eyes. "That was the most lifelike fake corpse I've ever seen. You're lucky you didn't break my windshield."

"I calculated the weight and speed of descent carefully." Cori rose to her full five feet with pride. "And they say math isn't useful in real life."

"There's a scavenger hunt to start," Bridget told the Reddings. "A getting-to-know-you sort of thing. Then a costume party fundraiser with an auction. And last, a race through a corn maze. We're still hoping for a haunted house." She looked at Cori. "How are we doing with that?"

Cori turned to Thelma. "We need a haunted house. Care to raise your hand?"

The librarian bristled. "I will not. I've given my library to the cause but I won't offer my home."

"We know a few people," I said. "But after all that's happened in Thistledown, I don't think anyone will throw open their doors."

Olive's arm was rising, its movement slow and jerky thanks to a boost from an orange sleeve. "I've got a haunted house," she said at last. "For real."

CHAPTER THREE

Thelma turned the sign on the library door to "closed," and said, "Lead the way, Miss Redding."

"Are you really going back to your maiden name, Olli?" Kestra asked. "It's weird to hear you described as 'Miss' again."

Olive pressed her lips together and then resolutely stepped into the lead. Her so-called haunted house was a short walk away. "Well, I'm not a 'Mrs.' anymore. My ex's actions made that clear and the paperwork formalized it recently."

A black glove came up with more than a slice of orange. "Too much information, Reddings. If you want to win one of our dogs, that is. Like I said earlier, we're looking for stable homes. Our rescues have been through the wringer and don't need more upheaval." Olive turned with color in her cheeks only to be hit with a patented Cori Hogan glare. "The haunted house isn't working in your favor, Olive."

"Maybe not, but I volunteered it. Transparency must count for something."

"In ghosts, it counts for everything," Edna said, chuckling. "Not that I've ever had the pleasure of meeting one."

"You won't today either," Cori said. "All that voodoo is a crock.

But we need a house with ghost appeal to stage our event. All the better if people actually think the threat is real."

Thelma pulled a colorful silk scarf from her suit pocket and tied it carefully over her curls to fight the fall dampness. It made a curious contrast with her black robes, and a woman crossed to the other side of the street. "I heard the scuttlebutt about your new house, Olive. What makes you think it's haunted?"

"A bad vibe," Olive said. "Funny noises. There's a strange scraping in the walls or overhead."

"That sounds more like a problem for an exterminator than an exorcist," Edna said, turning to Thelma. "Do you have an exorcist in Thistledown?"

The librarian patted her kerchief to ensure no curl remained exposed. "Not in the town proper, but I could drum up help elsewhere if the situation required."

Jilly's grim expression told me she had an idea where that help might reside. A situation at the schoolhouse library a few months ago had attracted interest from Janelle Brighton, Jilly's cousin, who lived in Wyldwood Springs and was purportedly a psychic. As with anything even remotely woo-woo, we didn't speak of it if it could be avoided. That didn't bother me in the slightest. There were plenty of things in my past I preferred not to discuss, even with my best friend. I respected her boundaries, she respected mine, and we both knew the door was open if we needed support.

Olive turned again. "I hired an exterminator and it didn't fix the problem. There were signs of pests, but nothing major. Last night I heard a... well, a jingle."

"A jingle?" Gertie asked. "A cheery ghost. Hard to get too worried about that." She nearly caught up with Olive, but the younger woman moved even faster. Perhaps proximity to Gertie's rifle, Minnie, was more worrisome than jingling in the walls.

"It's not just the noises." Olive's sigh wafted back to us. "Like I said, there's a bad vibe. It's the best way I can describe it. I wish I had visited the house before buying. I fell in love with it online and didn't want to see any flaws." She flicked her eyes at her sister and added, "I made the same mistake with my husband, I guess."

"He seemed like a good guy," Kestra said. "Handsome, too. Falling for him was understandable. The house, less so. It's an old wreck."

"With good bones. My agent said so. She told me I could fix it up nicely without spending too much."

"Ah, I see," Thelma said, as we turned the corner onto a narrow street lined with towering oak trees and just four houses. The trees were covered in leaves the color of drying blood. It was a shame I had enough experience to discern the many shades of red. "You bought the Sprocket place. It wasn't on the market long. Glennis Redding listed it low to sell quickly."

"I couldn't believe my luck finding something here I could afford," Olive said. "I'd set my heart on Thistledown. It seemed like such a quaint town. A great place to start over." Her fingers toyed with the zipper on her jacket, pulling it up six inches and then down again. "I wanted to get a job in a store to meet people while I figure out my next steps." She glanced at Thelma. "Being so close to the library was a selling factor."

"I try to serve as a community hub, but jobs are few and far between in Thistledown," Thelma said. "We're growing, but not as fast as some might wish. You'd be best to start your own business."

"I don't have the right—" Olive felt Cori's eyes on her and stopped. "Never mind. I have enough money to ride it out for a bit. And time on my hands."

"I hate to kick a gal when she's down, but Kestra is sounding like the better candidate despite her sorry taste in sweaters," Cori said. "Do you have gainful employment, Junior Redding? A roof over your head that isn't haunted?"

"I have a job and an apartment in Boston." Kestra kicked at the red leaves underfoot. "Not my dream job, but it pays the bills. I figure a dog would help me change the narrative."

"Change the narrative? What's that supposed to mean?" Cori asked.

I couldn't help jumping in. "Adopting a dog always changes the narrative, Cori. Every rescuer I know would say the same thing." She started to raise her glove and I waved it down. "Maybe these two would like some help from a former HR exec and the best headhunter Boston ever knew. Jilly and I can boost their confidence and their bottom line."

Kestra stared at me. "You just met us. Why would you take the trouble to do that?"

I gestured to Keats, and then Percy. The cat was dangling over Jilly's arm and staring at the Reddings with unblinking green eyes. "My pets like you. They say you're winners. That's true no matter who scores the Mafia's dogs."

Jilly's eyes, nearly as green as the cat's, finally found their twinkle. "Ivy and I loved helping people start over even before we found the change we needed."

"Two years ago, I got a new dog, a new home, the perfect calling and the man of my dreams," I said.

"Same," Jilly said. "Now we try to pay it forward."

I stopped at the foot of a long driveway. "First thing we need to do is figure out what's rattling around in this house. That's where I think my pets might help."

The "For Sale" sign was still planted in the lawn with the word "Sold" streaking across it. There were a few empty boxes at the side of the house, but the sign's continued presence told me Olive wasn't convinced about staying. Her feet slowed and she snapped the zipper up to her neck, confirming my suspicion. "How can your pets help?" she asked.

"If the problem is vermin, they'll know," Jilly said.

Olive's fingers left the zipper and rubbed her forehead. "And if it's a ghost?"

"It's not a ghost," Jilly said. "We don't believe in them."

"Speak for yourself," someone muttered behind me. I thought it was Thelma, but when I turned, her lips were sealed and she was folding her kerchief into a square.

"It's not a ghost." Edna weighed in on Jilly's side. "There's always a logical explanation for things that go jingle in the night."

"We'll find it and give you your dream house back," I said.

Cori flashed some glove. "Not so fast. We want to meet that ghost. How contestants react in the presence of specters will speak volumes about their capacity to care for one of our dogs. Rescues always bring surprises."

I looked down at Keats and it seemed like his blue eye winked deliberately. Since he'd dug a skull out from under the sunflowers in his first owner's yard, there hadn't been a single day without a surprise—some wonderful, others terrifying.

Edna became frustrated with the pace and stepped ahead of us. She held out her hand and when Olive dropped the key into it, my senior friend said, "I'm going in. Private Keats, you with me?"

My dog grumbled and I translated. "He thinks he's earned a promotion, Edna. Frankly, I agree. What comes above private in the apocalyptic army?"

"Corporal," Jilly said. "But I think he's at least a sergeant. Percy, too."

I caught a look between the Redding sisters. "Yes, we're always this weird," I said. "We'll grow on you."

Cori forged ahead with Edna. "Still waiting for that to happen." The tiny trainer thought of herself as a general in her own army, and Edna did, too. I was surrounded by confident leaders but the only one I followed wore a black-and-white fur tuxedo.

Keats trotted up the front steps and through the door Edna opened. Percy struggled to get down from Jilly's arms and then followed in leaps and bounds. They were excited about whatever this house had to tell us. A strange prickle started in my fingertips and crawled up my arms, leaving goosebumps behind. There were secrets here, obviously. As much as I depended on my pets to run interference with the mysteries we encountered, my own intuition wasn't too shabby.

Jilly rubbed her arms, suggesting she felt something strange, too. Since the pets had left us and charged ahead, I linked my arm through hers. I kind of expected the Reddings to do the same but there was a gap of nearly a yard between them. That distance hadn't varied much since I first saw them. They were together but apart, a feeling I knew well from my relationship with my own sisters.

Inside the house, our heels made an echoing sound on the worn hardwood flooring as we walked through the main floor. Olive had signaled not to bother removing our shoes—all the better to make a quick exit, I guessed. Despite the boxes outside, it didn't look like she'd unpacked many of her belongings. Or perhaps she wanted a really fresh start and hadn't brought much from her marital home. Either way, there was little to muffle the sound of our feet or perhaps a jingling intruder.

The realtor hadn't been wrong about the house having "good bones." Although I didn't know much about architecture, having lived in a condo before moving into Runaway Inn when it was freshly renovated, it seemed that someone had designed the place well. The windows were wide and deep, the rooms flowed easily from one to the next and there were elegant touches, like a compact fireplace surrounded by built-in bookshelves. In the dining room, I saw two stained glass windows, wainscoting and a plate rail that held only one large, ornate platter. With a little money or a lot of elbow grease, this house could be charming.

Remembering I wasn't house shopping but ghost hunting, I looked around for my pets. Keats stood between the living and dining rooms with his ruff slightly elevated.

"That's not good," Jilly muttered from close range. I'd barely noticed our arms were still linked. "Not ghost, but not good."

Percy was halfway up a rather grand staircase in the front hall. His tail had a decided bristle.

"Not good at all," I said, as we turned in unison to follow.

"What are you two muttering about?" Cori asked, staring with bright brown eyes that always reminded me of a crow's, or a fierce red-winged blackbird's.

"Nothing. We're heading upstairs," I said.

Orange fluff barred the doorway of the rear bedroom when we reached the landing. I sensed Percy didn't want to go in, and Jilly and I jammed in the doorway once he went inside. There was an impatient mumble behind us before Keats forced his way between our legs.

He walked a few yards and then stopped, one white paw rising in a point. There was nothing in the room except for a chest of drawers. Keats was directing us to the window. On the sill sat a very old doll with its little legs sticking straight out.

"Ew," Jilly said. "Creepy."

The doll was indeed creepy, with messy light brown hair, a white plaster face, rosy dots for cheeks, and pursed up lips. Her blue eyes would roll shut if you laid her on her back.

I knew this because I'd briefly owned a doll just like her. My mom had eloped from her childhood home and left nearly everything behind, but "Beauty," the doll, had come with her as part of her scanty trousseau. Beauty had dark hair, like Mom's, as well as the four daughters ahead of me who'd had custody of the doll. By the time Beauty landed in my arms, however, she was ready to retire. The elastic bands that attached her limbs and head to her torso snapped from old age and I was left cradling an armful of dismembered parts. I remembered the horror of clutching all the bits together, and then transferring them carefully into a cardboard shoebox coffin that I hid under my bed. It was months before I came clean and showed Mom what had happened to her first, and least troublesome, baby.

"Oh darling, don't worry," she'd said, as I sobbed. "Beauty did her time. She lasted longer than my marriage to your father. Just throw her in the trash."

Mom's eyes had filled, too, and only now did I realize that wasn't about the doll at all, but the dead marriage, or perhaps dead potential. Back then, I thought I had broken Mom's heart along with her doll. I didn't throw Beauty in the garbage. Instead, I asked my eldest sister, Daisy, to take care of her for me, in hopes of restoring her one day. I wouldn't be at all surprised to find that doll was stashed in Daisy's basement, neatly categorized with my neat-freak sister's label maker.

"What's wrong?" Jilly asked, as we followed Keats to the window. "I mean, aside from the creepy doll."

"Just a bad memory." I reached with my free hand for Keats. Normally he would sense my unease and offer his ears for comfort, but he was fixated on the doll or the window.

Looking past the doll and into the yard, I saw a garden full of orange pumpkins, most around the size of basketballs but some far larger. One had to be over three feet in diameter.

"Oh, how fun," Jilly said. "I love pumpkins, although I choose to associate them with Thanksgiving rather than Halloween."

We jumped as someone cleared her throat behind us. "It was the pumpkins that sold me," Olive said. "They were just starting to ripen when I found the place online. I saw them in the digital tour and found them so cheery."

I stared down at the orange orbs. Deceptively cheery, perhaps. I didn't trust botanical showiness anymore. "Let's go outside and take a closer look," I said.

CHAPTER FOUR

"Don't you want to see the master bedroom?" Olive asked, as Jilly and I followed the cat and dog downstairs. "I could hear the noises most clearly there."

"We'll circle back," I called over my shoulder. "After a quick look at the garden."

"What's so interesting about pumpkins?" she asked, rushing after us.

"It's Halloween." I slowed so she could catch up. "Pumpkins are the star attraction."

The pets turned and headed toward the kitchen but a knock at the front door stopped all of us.

Olive slipped around me and opened it, framing a woman in her early seventies. She had silvery blonde hair, a meticulous pumpkin-colored suit and bronze pumps and purse. Not everyone could pull off orange with panache, but this woman managed. Her eye shadow, blush and lipstick all had a bronze hue, too. I felt like I'd seen her somewhere before but couldn't quite put my finger on it.

"Hello, Glennis," Olive said. "I have guests at the moment. Could I give you a call later?"

Now I knew who she was. Glennis Redding's face was on huge

signs advertising her realtor services. Those billboards always seemed too much in the big city, but even more so stuck in farmer's fields or vacant lots around Thistledown. She had aged more than 20 years since her last professional photo shoot, but if I had to see my face at that scale, I'd shave a few off, too.

Glennis was about as subtle as her pumpkin suit. She tried to push past Olive into the front hall but confronted a tuxedoed barrier. "Stop that," she said, as Keats pushed her back out the door. "I do not need dog fur on my skirt. I plan to wear this when I award the rescue winners on Sunday morning."

"Keats, leave it." Taking over as lead sheepdog, I herded Glennis outside to the porch. He still wasn't satisfied and passed back and forth between us until the agent gave up and went down the stairs. "I'm sorry, Mrs. Tanner."

"Ms. Tanner. I kept my family name, much to my husband's dismay. My grandfather opened our realty over a hundred years ago and I've continued the legacy."

I went down the steps to keep Keats at bay. He was so determined to send Glennis on her way that he let Percy take the lead in exploring the pumpkin patch out back. There was a saucy flick of orange tail as the cat rounded the corner of the house.

"We're supposed to meet with my realtor tomorrow. Glennis," Olive said. "Paige asked me not to discuss the issue without her."

"But it's an urgent matter," Glennis said. "You raised spurious concerns about my clients, who sold you this house. I want to put the matter to rest today."

Olive seemed to shrink a little. "I'd like to wait for my agent, thanks."

Jilly stepped in front of Olive. "If that was the agreement, it's best to honor it, Ms. Tanner. Unless Olive wants to text Paige now and see if she's available."

Keats came back up the stairs and stared at Olive. I doubted she knew she was being herded with a blue-eyed stare, but she pulled out her phone nonetheless. "Fine, but we won't talk about putting things to rest until Paige gets here."

Glennis tried another advance on the stairs since Keats had retreated. "This house is not haunted, young lady. That's the most ridiculous thing I've ever heard. Maybe where you come from slandering a decent family's name is commonplace, but it doesn't happen in Thistledown."

"Sure, it does," I said. "I've spent enough time here to know that. Why don't we chat about the rescue event for a few minutes while we wait for Olive's agent to respond?"

The defiant set of Glennis's jaw told me she wanted to say her piece before Olive had adequate backup. Fortunately, she was vastly outnumbered. While Olive was forced off the porch by the rest of our party as they came out of the house, she was also surrounded. Edna and Gertie didn't need to know what the fuss was about to take objection to Glennis. Either the realtor's attitude or her loud suit rubbed my friends the wrong way. The feeling was mutual, judging by the contempt on Glennis's bronze-hued face.

"It's not Halloween yet," the realtor said, scanning Edna's camouflage. "It's funny how people lose their inhibitions at this time of year."

I raised my hand to stop Edna and Gertie from taking the bait. Glennis wanted to stir things up, probably to get Olive flustered and undermine her confidence and credibility. Whether or not the house was haunted, the new homeowner deserved her say.

"Don't be mean to my guests, Glennis," Olive said. "These are the organizers of the rescue event. They're doing a lot to bring attention to Thistledown."

Cori crossed her arms, arranging her gloves to put orange flares on display. "That's right, we are. And if you play your cards right, you may even find some new clients for your business. But don't be mean, Glennis. That's *my* purview."

"I'm not mean at all," Glennis said. "I gave Olive a lovely housewarming gift. A plate from my private collection and a treasure from the best antiques store in the region."

"The Langman Legacy?" I guessed. Glennis's nod made my stomach twist into a knot. Heddy and Kaye Langman broke the law more often than I did and were shameless about extorting such treasures from grieving families. One of them was obviously that ghastly doll. The housewarming gift that would haunt forever.

"Lovely gifts and I appreciate it." Olive's voice got stronger as a car pulled into the driveway behind Glennis's. "But let's stick to the matter at hand. Here's my agent, Paige Ogilvy."

"The matter at hand being a bogus haunting," Glennis said. She sucked in a breath and swelled visibly in preparation for the battle. Paige Ogilvy bounded out of the car ready to go for it, too. She was in her late forties but her hair cut and color were nearly identical to Glennis's. I couldn't help but wonder if Paige had deliberately modeled herself after the successful realtor. Her power suit was mustard-colored, however, which didn't pack quite the same punch. It also looked dated and her pumps had plenty of miles on them. "Paige, your claim is a crock of—"

"Glennis Redding, keep a civil tongue," Paige said. "It's a good thing I happened to be showing a house here and could head off your sneak attack at the pass. We had time booked tomorrow to sit down without an audience."

"Why don't we go around the back and give these folks some space?" Jilly said, motioning to our friends.

"I relish an audience," Glennis said, which was probably true of anyone who wore orange. She reminded me of my mother, who had a penchant for scarlet satin and attention. "Maybe it's normal for you to pull stunts to get out of a deal, Paige Ogilvy, but in Thistledown, your word is your bond."

Paige walked up to Glennis and their resemblance really was uncanny, despite the age difference. "Your client is the liar. The Sprockets initialed right beside the clause that said the place is ghost-free." She pulled out her phone, tapped a few times, and continued. "Let me summarize that clause for your audience."

"There's no need," Glennis said. "They wouldn't understand."

"Try us," Gertie said. "We're all quite bright, really."

Paige cleared her throat and then began. "The Seller warrants that to their knowledge and belief this property is not stigmatized. That implies no non-physical, intangible attribute of the property exists that may elicit a psychological or emotional response on the part of the buyer or—"

"I thought you were summarizing," Glennis interrupted.

Paige shot her a glare before continuing. "Or affect the value of the property. Such attributes include but are not limited to: crime scene, drug dealing, brothel, murder, suicide scene, previous ownership by notorious individual, haunted property and former grow-op."

"Well," Edna said. "That's certainly a mouthful. You must have taken elocution in public school, Paige."

Glennis's eyes were pinned on her doppelganger. "My clients stand behind their word. The Sprockets have no knowledge of the stigma you're alleging. If the house has acquired pests since the closing date, that's not our problem."

Olive lurched forward, suggesting a shove from behind from someone else who didn't hesitate to wear orange. "An exterminator said the house is clear. Of typical pests, anyway."

"My client hired that company at her own cost before agreeing to escalate the matter," Paige said. "Olive didn't want to cause a fuss, even though your clients ran for the hills. Quite literally. The Sprockets have gone about as far up the range as they can to avoid this place."

Glennis forged on, undeterred. "Distance doesn't protect reputation, as I'm sure anyone here can attest. My clients didn't run away but *get away* from the rat race." Her lips curled in a smile. "Speaking of which... I smell a rat. Your client is having buyer's remorse over what could only be a minor infestation."

"It's far from minor," Paige said. "Olive is extremely stressed by what's happening in this house and that's grounds to nullify the contract."

"You want to give the place back, Olli?" Kestra asked. "I thought this was your dream house."

Olive shrugged. "It was my dream to find something affordable in Thistledown so I'd have enough left over to make it my own. Now we know why this house was a steal. Someone died here. I can sense it."

"No one died here," Glennis said. "Your 'psychological and emotional response' comes from your personal problems, not the house."

Thelma had been uncharacteristically quiet but she stepped forward now. "The house is very old, Glennis. At least half a dozen people have been carted out in pine boxes. That's a matter of public record."

The pumpkin suit deflated slightly in the face of Thelma's superior knowledge. "Only in the normal course of events. People inevitably transition to the hereafter. There was no reason for any of those people to, you know..."

"Stick around and spook things up?" Cori suggested, grinning. "Here's the thing, Glennis. I don't know much about real estate, but I know plenty about corruption in hill country. Isn't it possible one of those pine boxes left a criminal shadow behind?"

"No, it is not possible. There is nothing in the public record about criminal activity in this house." Her eyes cut to Thelma. "Is there?"

"Not to my knowledge," Thelma admitted. "But if there's one thing I've learned as the town's de facto historian, it's that criminals don't always get caught. Especially the skilled ones."

Glennis stood a little taller on her bronze heels. "Well, the burden of proof is on the new owner to establish there's anything more at play here than raccoons or squirrels. I wish you luck in proving there's a ghost."

The realtors' voices rose and the crowd closed in around them. I found myself moving away from the conflict, albeit unknowingly. Keats had insinuated himself in front of Jilly and me, pressing us back so gradually we didn't notice until he turned us to face each other. My best friend nodded and we let the dog herd us around the side of the house and into the back yard.

At first it was hard to pick out Percy among the pumpkins, some about the same size as my orange cat. However, his movements gave him away before Keats went into a point.

"Oh Percy, don't," Jilly called as we walked across the grass. "You've got a perfectly good litterbox in the truck that you prefer to regular dirt. There's no need to sully Olive's pumpkins."

The cat's sweeping became more flamboyant. Either the earth was packed hard, or he was signaling something less mundane than a potty call.

Jilly must have come to the same conclusion because we picked up speed with no encouragement from Keats.

The voices grew louder as the bickering crowd followed us into the back yard. By this point, I was bent over the pumpkin patch with Jilly, and she clutched my arm.

"Paige, for goodness' sake," Glennis trumpeted. "Give it up."

"What is that cat doing?" Paige asked, coming over to the garden. "Olive doesn't need a feline nuisance on top of the supernatural one."

Glennis followed, grumbling loudly. "There is absolutely nothing funny afoot here."

She was half right. There was nothing funny about the situation, but there was most definitely a foot here.

And both agents screamed when they saw it.

CHAPTER FIVE

"That's a fake," Glennis said, backing away quickly. "Skeletons are hanging all over town for Halloween. What a shame local youth buried a surprise to prank the newcomer."

Edna came over to inspect Percy's discovery. "The problem is that we've seen a variety of skeletons before. Some fake, others all too real. This foot falls into the latter category."

"That's ridiculous." Glennis's own feet were moving faster than a prank warranted. "You don't know what you're talking about."

Straightening, Edna patted her perm. "No? I would have thought a long career in nursing qualified me to know human remains when I saw them. I took every bonus training offered, including an overly long stint in a morgue."

"I've never done a stint in a morgue but I have had occasion to see and even carry old bones," I said. "This foot is the real thing. The only question is why it's here."

"And to whom it belonged," Edna added. "Another important question."

"How very tragic," Paige said, pulling a packet of tissues from her purse. She plucked one out with trembling fingers and pressed it to her nose. "An atrocity occurred here."

"It's long past smelling, madam," Edna said. "Well over fifty years, by my estimation."

Paige didn't move the tissue. "Since this body didn't leave in a pine box, or have a box at all, I suppose he's the one haunting the house. He wants justice. And so does my client."

Now halfway across the yard, Glennis regained some wind in her suit. "Just because there's a body in the pumpkin patch doesn't mean there's a ghost in the house. Regardless, the Sprockets clearly had nothing to do with it. If this"—she flicked her fingers at Edna— "morgue lady is correct in her estimate, my clients probably weren't even born when such a dreadful thing transpired. I'll bet this fellow tumbled in there while gardening and was never found."

Edna, Gertie and a few others laughed, my dog among them.

That earned an admonishing stare from Jilly. "Stop. It's not funny." Her eyes fell on Percy, who was still making half-hearted sweeps. Picking him up, she moved away. "I'm quite sure this person —man or woman—didn't fall into the garden while planting pump-kins. But that isn't for us to determine. I'll call the police now."

"Yes, do," Paige said, still holding the tissue to her nose. "And while the police investigate, Glennis and I can arrange to dissolve the deal. Olive was distressed before and now she'll be traumatized."

Olive looked more stunned than traumatized. She stood among the others, and it wasn't her sister who draped an arm over her shoul-ders to comfort her, but Bridget Linsmore. To be fair, Kestra looked equally stunned. The majority of us—even Cori and Bridget—had encountered death before. Some bad ends were more daunting than others. If push came to shovel, I'd take an old skeleton any day. I'd carried a skull and a femur in my handbag on two different occasions and managed reasonably well by using Glennis's strategy—specifi-cally, telling myself they were plastic. I didn't deliberately delude myself often, but when it came to transporting old bones, it did more good than harm.

Luckily there was no cause to transport this foot, or the rest of the bones sticking out of the soil. Percy must have cleared more dirt away while we were talking because I hadn't noticed fingers earlier. Or the slight curve of a damaged skull. A tingle danced up my spine like a tarantula. Surely those bones weren't emerging on their own. This wasn't a horror movie, however much it was beginning to feel like one.

I turned away from the garden but the prickling of the imaginary tarantula intensified and I had to look back.

"Mesmerizing, isn't it?" Thelma asked, joining me. "And no, it's not moving. That's an optical illusion brought on by shock."

We probably weren't alone in experiencing it. Everyone had drifted except for Edna and Gertie. Cori, Bridget and the Reddings were lined up against the fence. For all the terrible rescue situations the Mafia faced, even Cori quailed when it came to scenes like this.

"I can't stay here," Olive said, tears filling her eyes. "This house really was too good to be true."

Paige called over, "Don't you fret. We'll get your money back and find you something without a history."

"In Thistledown?" Thelma asked. "Good luck. We're as steeped in crime as most hill country towns. Perhaps more so, being an older outpost. The police will have their work cut out for them sorting through a stack of cold cases higher than the roof."

My eyes drifted up with the word and caught a movement in a small window under the eaves.

"What?" Edna said. "You look like you saw a ghost. *The* ghost."

"There's no ghost," Glennis called, seeming to monitor every conversation.

I shook my head. "Looked like movement in the attic window, but I'm sure it was nothing. A few minutes ago I thought the skeleton was digging itself out of the ground."

Forcing my lips into a smile, I reached for Keats and found his ears waiting. His bristling fur suggested I hadn't been wrong about the attic, but there was no point alarming Olive any further by sharing my dog's opinion that something lurked upstairs. Perhaps something that jingled in the night.

Edna pressed in, no doubt intending to query me, but sirens deterred her. "That was fast." She sounded disappointed. "I count on the cops around here to be as slow as decomp in a hill country winter."

"We didn't even have a designated officer until I was held hostage in my own library," Thelma said. "After that, we got more attention." She gave me a wry smile, as I'd had a key role in that incident. "I don't know as I feel any safer with Officer Wiebe at the helm."

"Jacob Wiebe? I think I met him at a wedding," I said, watching Percy thrash his way out of Jilly's grip. "The guy looked like a teenager."

"Not far off," Thelma said. "Jacob was a regular in the library's extracurricular activities, which is something. But I don't think he's ready for such responsibility on his own."

Keats nudged my leg and I took his prompt. "Lucky for the newbie officer, he has a seasoned team to support his work." I gestured around our immediate circle. "We're in the right place at the right time."

Jilly shook her head as she put her phone away. "Bet he won't see it that way. If he's new and keen he'll want to prove himself with this case."

"Do you think you've taught me nothing, my friend?" I asked, grinning. "Took me ages, but I finally realized it's better not to show up the cop in charge."

"Especially if he's your boyfriend. Or fiancé." She grinned back, and it was heartening to see. "Or husband, for that matter."

Edna blew out a raspberry. "I look forward to the day you girls stop indulging the male ego. I don't intend to soft-pedal our skills around this youngster in charge. If he's old enough to hold a badge, he's old enough to learn from his betters. He'll take our help and be grateful."

I laughed. "When has that ever happened with a cop we know? Even when they're grateful, they're not."

Jilly laughed, too, but honesty forced her to add, "We've been known to complicate police business."

"Mainly for expedience," Edna said. "While the police do their legal do-si-do, we take the shortest route to get a killer off the streets. Personally, I think we deserve to be honored in a public ceremony. With medals. Trophies would be too cumbersome to carry into a bunker."

"I'll put in a good word with Mayor Martingale," I said. "But don't hold your breath."

Paige was still holding hers, judging by the tissues in her hand and the florid color in her cheeks. Glennis, on the other hand, looked pale under her bronze blush and both agents were silent for a change.

Cori had started to move around the yard, gloves shoved in her pockets. It was rare that her orange flares were silenced, but it wasn't long before a spark appeared in her birdlike eyes. "Ivy. Look sharp. Someone's trying to tell you something."

That someone was Percy. He was on the sill of what I presumed to be the kitchen window. We hadn't finished our tour of the house. The cat's back was arched and he was hissing.

"Is he silly enough to hiss at his own reflection?" Glennis asked.

Edna was the first to jump to Percy's defense. "That cat was the second smartest cat in my feral colony. Saved my life then and Ivy's half a dozen times afterward."

"More," I said. "Along with Keats and assorted other guest-starring animals." I walked to the window. "Percy would not hiss at his reflection."

"But he might at a ghost," Paige called, through a tissue. "Now that we've found the body, that specter is as bold as brass."

"It's not a ghost," Glennis insisted, her voice brassy, too.

In this, she was right. Percy was nearly apoplectic for a more mundane reason. On the other side of the glass a black feline was giving him catitude.

Lifting my own warrior down from the ledge, I turned to Olive. "You didn't mention owning a cat."

"Cinders, yes. She's pretty much been in hiding since I moved into the house two weeks ago. Mostly only comes out in the night to eat. But she hasn't caught a mouse yet and she's always been a good hunter."

The movement I'd noticed in the attic window made sense now. Cinders probably spent her time up there and came down to confront Percy.

Keats brushed against my shins to back me away from the window. His mumble suggested my attention would be better spent elsewhere. Not the pumpkin patch, thank goodness. Instead, he led me to the back of the yard and lifted his paw in a point. I knelt to stare into the grass, which was still quite green thanks to a mild fall. Pulling a penknife out of my pocket, I prodded the grass aside and then the sun glinted off silver. It was a charm in the shape of a skull with tiny red chips for eyes. The chain it had hung on snaked through the grass beside it. I used my phone to blow it up for a closer look.

"Hey!" A male voice boomed out over the murmur of women's voices in the yard. "Step away from the evidence, Ivy Galloway. This is my case."

Keats mumbled some advice that morphed into a pant-laugh.

"Oh dear," I mumbled back as I took a quick photo. "The only thing worse than a cop with something to prove is a cop *brother* with something to prove."

CHAPTER SIX

A sher was dropping a kiss on Jilly's cheek when I straightened. No matter how much responsibility he assumed, he never forgot for a second how lucky he was to have my best friend as his bride. It was hard to believe it had already been a year since they tied the knot in the apple orchard at Runaway Farm.

"What are you doing here, brother?" I asked, walking back to them. "I thought you were deployed to some undercover project in—"

He raised an official hand. "Undercover means keep a lid on it, sis. What we discuss at the dinner table doesn't go any further."

Sometimes it was a struggle to remember he was no longer the goof who leapt out of dark corners wearing fright masks. Well, the problem was that he was still that goof, and would love nothing more than to make me jump and scream. But he was also a cop-on-the-rise, who'd run lead on a couple of high-profile investigations lately. Kellan made sure Asher had all the challenge he wanted while still being able to orbit the farm like a satellite. I appreciated the added layer of protection, but it meant I forfeited autonomy at home, and now, apparently in other towns.

"Are you here to help the Thistledown officer?" I asked. "I heard he's new to the job."

"New to the job, but not the community," a uniformed man said, coming up behind my tall brother. "I'm Jacob Wiebe. Chief Harper offered support from a skilled investigator when he heard about a potential murder. Thank you, Galloway."

"You're welcome." My voice overlapped with Asher's, although I knew full well the young officer meant my brother.

"No problem," Asher said, scowling at me. "I was in the neighborhood."

"Ma'am, I'm sorry." Officer Wiebe looked abashed. "Chief Harper sort of said the opposite about you."

"What?" I feigned indignation. "My fiancé knows I'm a skilled investigator."

"I took a quick look at your file, ma'am, and noticed you stole a police vehicle right here in Thistledown last fall."

"My brother's vehicle," I pointed out. "You could say I borrowed his car for an hour for important pet-related business and happened to disable a killer in the process."

"It's true, JJ," Thelma said, coming up beside me. "We also saved a reporter's life. I presume that's noted in your file, too."

"Jacob, Miss Tilrow. No one calls me JJ anymore. And I'd ask you to call me Officer Wiebe in my formal capacity. Or just sir."

Thelma laughed. "Good for you, young man. I always appreciated that you handled library materials with care. Perhaps I should have anticipated your new career from your old obsession with the 'Piggy Solves the Crime' series."

The young man had the worst kind of blush—the splotchy maroon variety. It was impossible to hide and would be helpful as I assisted my brother in solving this case. Undercover, of course. So undercover that Asher wouldn't even notice if I could help it.

I couldn't always help it. The brother who greeted me warmly when I came back to the region was a sweet, gullible overgrown boy.

The handsome man before me now was more savvy and harder to fool. Kellan and Jilly shared much of the credit for that, but I liked to believe that trying to outmaneuver his sleuthing sister had a role to play in helping Ash level up. What's more, it leveled me up, too. I doubted I could steal my brother's squad car today, but I'd still enjoy trying.

Asher was watching me closely, and worse, watching Keats and Percy. What I might be able to hide from him, my pets could not. The dog wasn't big on guile around my family, and Percy couldn't be bothered. Even my brother could see the boys were restless and unsettled. Both had the puffy signs of trouble in the works.

The brother of a year ago would have dismissed it as nothing and moved on. Today, he said, "What's wrong with the boys? Looking testy."

"They just found a body in the pumpkin patch," Jilly answered for me. "Isn't that enough to make anyone testy?"

"An old skeleton, from the sounds of it," he said. "Jacob?"

Officer Wiebe walked over to the garden and crouched to take a look. When he looked back up, his mottled blush had drained completely away. He was naturally very pale and looked even more so surrounded by pumpkins. "Just a bunch of bones."

Asher looked from his wife to me. "Discovering a bunch of old bones would normally be a happy score for Keats and Percy. What aren't you telling me, Ivy?"

I was glad he directed the question to me, because Kellan often spoke straight to the dog and read his reactions with increasing accuracy. My fiancé had always been harder to evade than my brother, but Kellan's willingness and ability to interpret the pets' behavior made it nearly impossible now. That didn't stop me from trying, either. As a former HR exec, I appreciated motivation for continuous improvement.

Before I could answer, Paige Ogilvy came over and moved her tissue aside to enunciate clearly. "What she's not telling you is that this house is haunted. My client, Olive Redding, was unaware of that fact when she took ownership two weeks ago. She was traumatized even before this grisly garden discovery."

"It's not haunted," Glennis said. "And my clients, the Sprockets, had no awareness of these bones."

"It's haunted," Paige said.

I wasn't sure what was going on in that house. As a rule, I didn't believe in such things, but I'd also encountered situations I couldn't explain away rationally. My go-to response to the inexplicable was close observation paired with logic. Only if those left me high and dry would I entertain less plausible theories. Going straight to ghost felt almost like cheating. Besides, it took the power out of my hands. There was nothing I could do about haunting and that took all the fun out of sleuthing.

"Haunted?" My brother's blue eyes darted around and I saw opportunity. He was savvier but talk of ghosts took him out of his comfort zone—even more so because it took Jilly out of hers. "That's highly unlikely. Seems like Halloween is going to everyone's head."

"Definitely," Jilly said. "I'm sure Olive's cat is behind any strange activity in the house."

I looked at Olive and her hair swished a slight negative. She probably knew her cat as well as I knew mine, and this was outside normal parameters. However, it was a new house, and that was cause to unsettle pets as well as humans. It had taken a long time to feel at home at the inn, and that would have been true even without a couple of murders on my property.

"We'll take a close look," Asher said. "And go over the yard with a fine-tooth comb. I can't imagine we'll find much evidence considering the crime is decades old."

"You don't know it's a crime," Glennis said. "Maybe a previous owner wanted to keep loved ones close to home. Many hill country founders had family graveyards. My great-grandparents certainly did and my grandfather was angry when the township banned the practice."

Thelma saved my brother from responding. "Glennis, I highly doubt your great-grandfather dumped his relatives into a hole in the yard without so much as a coffin, let alone a marker. Anyone who had a family graveyard treated their dearest with respect."

Cori directed both index fingers at Glennis like pistols. "First you suggested a gardening accident. Now it's a family graveyard?"

"A gardening accident?" My brother's lips twitched. Despite his personal growth of late, his sense of humor was never far from the surface. It was wonderful in a brother and a little tricky in a cop. "Doubtful," he said. "I checked the system and no one reported a missing gardener at this address. Or anyone else for that matter."

"But there is a long list of missing people in the area," Thelma said. "You're free to avail yourself of my records if there are gaps in those of the police."

"I'm sure our records are more comprehensive than yours, Miss Tilrow." Officer Wiebe sounded rather severe. He wanted to show her how far he'd come since crime-solving with Piggy.

Asher glanced from me to Thelma. "Not necessarily, Wiebe. I've learned that librarians know plenty. We'll stop by, Miss Tilrow."

Her stiff curls inclined slightly at his show of deference. "Please do."

"The rest of you... clear out," Asher said. "With all due respect, honey."

Jilly smiled at him. "My pleasure. We have a rescue event to run."

He churned his hair with his fingers, as he always did when he had to disagree with her. "You'll need to press pause on that until we've assessed this situation."

Cori's pistols came up again and took aim at my brother. This time there was orange in the barrel. "You don't press pause on an event like this, Officer Smiley. We've been planning it for months and people are coming from all over hill country to watch. Can you assess the sitch pronto? We need the haunted house tomorrow. On Halloween."

Asher rarely prickled at barbs from Cori, but his back stiffened now. "I don't take requests about policing from pet rescuers, Ms. Hogan. The investigation will unfold with all due diligence."

"We can find another suitable house," Bridget said. "It can't be the only one in the area."

Cori pouted. "I like this one. It has creep factor. Most of our contestants won't make it through here, and our selection will be dead easy." She smirked. "Poor choice of words."

Glennis stared at Cori. "You're a strange little woman."

"Says the woman dressed like a pumpkin who suggested a flowery fatality," Cori said. "But I've been called worse."

Asher spread his arms and flapped, like a brawny scarecrow. The gesture made me smile, as it was something my dignified fiancé would never do. "Go. All of you," he said. "We have a murder to investigate. I'll make some calls and get back to you about the rescue event."

Jilly caught his wrist and one wing dropped instantly. "It's an old crime, Asher. Since there's no current threat, surely it won't impede a themed event? As silly as I find Halloween, people love it and it will bring in a lot of money for rescue."

"Not to mention tourism dollars to our town," Glennis said.

Thelma merely pursed her lips, as if an influx of people was a dubious gift.

"Go," Officer Wiebe said, imitating Asher's flapping. There were other gestures he'd be better copying from my brother. "I've got this."

Keats directed a nip at Jacob's uniformed pant leg as we left the yard and mumbled a gripe to anyone in earshot. Jilly's eyes met mine before bending to pick up Percy. We both understood that Officer Wiebe and probably even Asher didn't "have this."

But Keats did. And that was good enough for now.

CHAPTER SEVEN

My phone rang a few hours later as I walked along Main Street with my assigned rescue contestants, Olive Redding and Nigel Byrd, a handsome but quiet man close to my age. Falling back, I greeted Kellan cheerily. "Happy nearly-Halloween!"

"You hate Halloween," he said. "Or at least you did earlier in the week. I've been told women are changeable but I hate buying into a cliché."

"That's just the thing. I decided to buy into a cliché and get the most out of this event. People love it so I must be missing something. I hereby commit fully to Halloween."

He laughed. "And what exactly does that entail?"

"First, enjoying the spoils. Thistledown is full of delicious treats. Nothing to rival Mandy's yet, but I keep an open mind."

I had a candy apple in a small plastic bag but didn't think I could manage to take a bite while talking to my beloved. Instead, I stuck my nose inside and pulled in a deep breath of my youth. There wasn't much I remembered fondly from Halloween, but the smell of a candy apple was one of them. Another was the aroma of the sugary treats I collected around the neighborhood and stashed in a plastic pumpkin. I ate my favorites first and worked through the treat hierarchy until only the nasty tasteless toffee was left. That I bartered with Asher, who normally had double or triple my haul. He dressed for speed in a superhero costume and headed out with similarly athletic friends. They took the streets of Clover Grove by storm, changing masks and outfits so they could hit the best houses repeatedly.

It still surprised me that my brother ended up on the right side of the law.

"So, you and Jilly are on a culinary tour of the town?" Kellan asked. "That sounds nice. And uncharacteristic, given what you found this morning."

"Actually, Jilly and I split up. We have a commitment to the rescue event."

"Asher hasn't given the event the go-ahead," Kellan reminded me.

"He will. Cancelling affects too many people and animals." Finally I snuck a bite of the candy apple and regretted it as my upper lip stuck to my front teeth. "And fits a bold dime."

"Pardon me?"

I managed to free my teeth with an unromantic sucking sound. "Sorry. I said it's an old crime."

"What are you eating that's gumming up the works?"

"Candy apple. Trying to get into the spirit of things."

"Never liked those. And don't much like that you're going ahead without official sanction from the man in charge."

"See, here's the thing. Jilly told Ash we were going on a scavenger hunt and he didn't say no. That means, yes, right?"

"Not when I'm running lead, but it's his party."

I took a careful bite of apple, decided it was better in theory than reality and threw the rest in a trash can. Hopefully a squirrel would get my money's worth out of it. "I hate scavenger hunts. It's the type of team-building activity I made staff do when I worked in HR. That was when I thought I was a people person."

He laughed again. "Were you ever? A people person?"

"Nope. I sure picked the wrong field for my personality. I'm more interested in my bickering goats than people."

"And yet you have more friends than anyone else I know."

"Because they all hate team building, too. That bonds us."

"I follow you. Many couldn't, but I do. It seems like Cori would hate team building, too."

I dug a piece of fudge in the shape of a bat out of my purse. "She sure does. This is part of thinning the flock. We're supposed to get to know people and vote them off the island if they're unworthy of a Mafia dog."

"And your charges?"

Confirming Olive and Nigel were still out of earshot, I continued. "I've got Olive Redding, and so far I like her. She's the one who owns the supposedly haunted house. Considering what's going on, she's been great. The guy is a mystery so far. Looks good and says little."

"Looks good? Should I be jealous?"

"Never." I took a bite of fudge and it went down easier than the apple. "Besides, I think he might have a crush on Olive. He doesn't say much but I'm picking up a vibe."

"And Olive? What does she think?"

I took another bite of fudge and then dropped it back in my bag. The problem with Mandy is that she'd spoiled me for perfectly good confections. Asher would likely take this overly sweet bat off my hands later. Toothmarks never fazed him. Sharing was caring in a family our size.

"Olive is fresh out of a nasty breakup, and not even ready for a rebound. Nigel would be better directing his eyes at the younger Redding. I think Kestra's hand-knitted orange Halloween sweater might have scared him off."

"It would certainly scare me off," he said. "Your new interest in Halloween is unnerving enough."

"Blame it on Thelma. When she pointed out how much the community loves it, I had to rethink. I've been a Halloween scrooge before now. I won't promise to love it forever but I'm giving it my all till the rescue coffers are full. Bring on the witches and skeletons. At least of the plastic variety." I flicked my fingers at Keats to rein in my little group, who were getting too far ahead. Having a sheepdog on a mission like this was a big advantage. Jilly would have her hands full with just Percy as her assistant, especially if her contestants showed more spark. Mine were just plodding along like... well, sheep. "Any idea who owned the real bones?"

"None. Unfortunately, the stack of unsolved cases in Thistle-down rivals ours. We need a better idea of dates just to narrow it down. At this point, there are close to thirty possibilities."

"Thirty? That's nothing. How about we split up that list and zip through it real quick?"

"Officer Wiebe would be heartbroken to lose the first interesting case he's seen so far. Asher is mostly lending Jacob a helping hand."

"To identify a mystery foot. You know I have experience tracking the origins of old bones. There are better ways to spend my time than checking off a scavenger hunt list."

"I know, but I've been asked to build policing capacity across the region. If you stubbornly refuse to attend cop college, you leave me no choice but to bench you."

"I'd get kicked out of cop college. First one to go. You know that."

He tried to muffle a snicker and failed. "You don't respond well to authority, and cop college is all about proving you do. Or at least can."

"I can." Keats came back for me, circled, and gave me a poke in the calf to get moving. "In fact, I'm responding to authority now. Officer Keats is rounding me up. Do you hear me objecting?"

"Well, I'm glad he's engaged in team building. It'll keep you safer."

I dodged my dog on the sidewalk so I could finish my conversation. No matter how often I talked to Kellan, it was never enough. "We're safe. A pile of bones in a garden doesn't pose much of a threat."

He sighed. "Sometimes when you start poking around pumpkin patches it can raise old ghosts. Isn't that how Halloween lore goes?"

"I guess." Keats circled again and I ducked around a planter filled with orange chrysanthemums. "Speaking of ghosts, when can I get into Olive Redding's place? I suspect the noises she heard come from an animal and I want to make sure it's safe. Especially if the Mafia gets to turn the house into a frightening attraction. They're set on having a haunted house to eliminate the weakest contestants and reveal the winners."

"Again, not up to me. I left this in your brother's capable hands and won't undermine him."

"Not fair," I said. "Ash will come down on me with a heavy hand just to prove something to the young upstart."

"And maybe to protect you and his wife," Kellan said. "It's coming from a good place. A brotherly place."

"Says the man with no siblings. Asher routinely scared the life out of me at Halloween and taxed my candy haul down to the inferior treats."

I could sense Kellan shaking his head. "I always wanted a brother, you know. Or even a sister. Thank you for curing me of that blighted wish."

"Oh, it wasn't all bad. I learned valuable lessons from navigating my clan."

In this case, I'd learned to feign great love for the candy I hated so that Asher would seize it and leave me what I really liked. In short, I learned how to live a lie when the stakes were high—skills that would stand me in good stead now, when I had to get around him. In his bratty youth, he'd trained me for this very task.

"And now I'm learning valuable lessons from navigating your

clan," Kellan said. "It's harder at this age. My brain isn't as flexible as it once was."

"You're discerning now. When I was learning at Asher's boots, my brain was a sponge. I didn't know the good from the bad. Let's not even discuss what I picked up from Poppy. Thank goodness she wanted little to do with Asher and me. We were sort of an island back then. The afterthoughts." Another tug on my jeans brought me back from the brink of sadness. "Ooh, look. Marshmallow ghosts. That's on our list."

"The list for what? Dental trauma?"

"My team is totally going to nail this scavenger hunt. Thanks to Keats, we've checked off half the items already."

"Pet rescue as a competitive sport?"

"That's the whole point. There are way more contestants than dogs. Someone's going home disappointed and it won't be Olive Redding if I can help it. She'll need a good dog if she decides to stay in that house. She got it for a song and there's nothing comparable on the market. The low listing price tells me the previous owners knew there was some kind of problem. They wanted out at any cost."

"Maybe, but a few other places have gone for less than market price over the years. I had my eye on Thistledown when I was thinking about flipping my house. There are some old gems there I wanted to polish."

That made me smile. "Before you realized your true love was farm maintenance."

His laugh was warm enough now to take the chill out of a fall day. "I realized my true love had the good sense to hire skilled help so that we could indulge other hobbies together."

"Exactly. Like crime-solving, and yet—"

"Ivy, if you want Asher to let you help, you'll need to use your little sister mojo on him." Before I could reply, he added, "And leave me out of it. I hate family politics."

"Understood, Chief. I'll fulfill my obligations to rescue and then see how Asher's doing. By then he might be appropriately grateful for my help."

"I wouldn't count on that. Remember, while he stole your candy, you stole his squad car. In the Thistledown area. He's been desperate to rehab his rep among his peers there. Now's his chance."

"I hear you, Chief. But I also hear an urgent mumble telling me to grab that marshmallow ghost before it's gone."

"Call me later?"

"I will. Ow!" The phone popped out of my hand and I barely heard Kellan's voice as it plummeted to the pavement.

It sounded like, "Better you than me."

CHAPTER EIGHT

M ain Street in Thistledown was flexing its style muscles. When I began spending time here a year ago, it was pretty, if unoriginal. Like many hill country destinations, it fashioned itself after Dorset Hills, with quaint signage featuring only slight variations on color and font. With each visit, however, the town seemed to gain confidence and now they worked a theme so hard it perspired twinkle lights. With the sun fading early, those orange and white strings were a welcome spark in the late afternoon. We only had four things left on our scavenger list and I was reasonably sure we'd trounce our opponents.

Granted, Keats and I were pretty much carrying the weight. Olive Redding was willing and agreeable, but she kept drifting away into her thoughts. Considering all that had happened, it was understandable. Nigel Byrd was also agreeable, but despite my best efforts, I couldn't get much out of him. My interviewing skills normally loosened tongues but today I was shooting blanks. Both contestants would need to amp things up if they hoped to "sell" Cori Hogan. She was the gatekeeper to Bridget and more importantly, Beau, the elegant dog who made the final decision on placements. It's not that

Cori valued chitchat, but conversation revealed much about a potential dog owner's competence.

Near the end of the strip of stores, I surrendered the scavenger list to Olive. "I already own the best dog in the world. Over to you guys if you want to win this competition."

Olive's lips sagged into a frown. "I'm not as confident as I was when I signed up two weeks ago. Back then, I had a house with a nice yard and prospects for work. Nobody's going to want to hire me now. I'll be known as the one with the haunted house and bones in the yard. People will forget the place came that way."

"Sounds like you've been the victim of small-town gossip before," I said. "I've been on the wrong side of the rumor mill more times than you can imagine. Yet I'm still smiling. At least most of the time."

She pulled her long hair into a ponytail. No matter how hard I tried, mine was never that sleek. "You're practically a celebrity for putting criminals away, whereas I made a bad choice and ended up marrying one. And another bad choice in buying a house that I knew was too good to be true."

I looked around for Nigel and found him staring into a store called Every Witch Way. Its window display featured crystals, wind chimes and stained glass ornaments. His clothes were so conservative I doubted this was his kind of place. Perhaps he was being kind and giving Olive a moment to vent.

"I've made plenty of bad choices," I told Olive. "But I try to keep an open mind and especially an open heart. That's where I figure my strength lies... in friendship and family. You're lucky to have your sister."

"Kestra and I aren't close. She's only here because she wants to win a dog, too."

"Nothing wrong with that. It's something you have in common."

Olive stared at the list and then at a grocery store across the street. "We're practically strangers. Like I mentioned earlier, our grandmother adopted Kestra when she was a baby, because Mom was sick. Then our brother came along and he was sick, too. Not sure if Gran chose to keep Kess or Mom insisted, but either way, she grew up in a flat at Howler Hall. It must have been so fun."

Keats circled Olive and redirected her to the store Nigel had targeted. "Olive, it was probably difficult for Kess to be raised apart from her siblings," I said. "I felt isolated enough as the last of six. I always knew my mom wanted to stop earlier."

There was a determined set to her jaw and she turned back to the grocery store. She had made up her mind about this a long time ago and it wouldn't be changed by a stranger and her persistent sheepdog. "I bet we can find a piñata over there."

"Or here," Nigel said, motioning to the store with the crystals. "I saw someone coming out with one earlier. It was shaped like a pumpkin."

Olive winced and Nigel looked sorry he'd strung so many words together. But Keats cast the deciding vote and herded them up the stairs. His ears had flattened, suggesting the fun was fast draining out of scavenging. I felt the same.

Inside, Olive circled the perimeter of the store and Nigel went in the opposite direction. I took Keats' cue and went straight to the counter to greet the woman bent over an accounts book. Her long gray hair hung in strings that couldn't decide between curly and straight. She used her hair like a bead curtain to block me out.

"May I help you?" she said at last, lifting her pencil from the ledger. No fancy tech spreadsheets for her.

"Yes, please. We're in the market for a candle that smells like pumpkin spice, a white spider and a bat ornament."

"And a piñata," Olive called.

The storekeeper let her glasses slip down her nose. "That's quite a list. Do you really think that dynamo with the orange-fingered gloves would make it that easy? You can't tick off four items in one place."

I shrugged. "Worth a try. This gentleman saw someone leave with a piñata shaped like a pumpkin."

The woman turned her cool stare on Nigel. "That was the last one."

A mumble from Keats suggested otherwise. I couldn't imagine he knew what a piñata was but he had a good ear for a lie, even when both ears were flat against his head. He didn't like this woman at all.

I pointed to the doorway into the back room. "Maybe there's one in there. Pretty sure I see a pumpkin that looks ready to rain goodies on aspiring rescue dog owners."

"The last one's on hold." She yanked a curtain across the doorway. "Piñatas are for kids, anyway. Not adults playing childish games."

There was a plaque on the wall behind her, and a photo with a local dignitary. At some point, Blenda Mushing had been cited for civic spirit, which had clearly drained away. Resting my hands on the counter, I tried to catch her eyes. They were the palest blue I'd ever seen. "I'm not a big fan of Halloween for grown-ups, either, Ms. Mushing, but it's not for me to question how this competition works." Tapping the glass case with my fingertips, I added, "It does seem like you cater to the trick-or-treater in all of us. Like my store-keeper friend says, Halloween is a retail holiday."

Blenda's eyes narrowed and came in for a landing. "I take spirituality seriously year-round."

"I can see that," I said. "I love these silver charms. The witch is adorable. Do you have a skull with red eyes?"

"Witches are never adorable. That's offensive. And I ran out of skulls. There was a rush on them today after what happened. It's all anyone can talk about."

Olive turned, her expression dour. "I just wanted a fresh start in Thistledown."

"Such a shame there's something stale in your pumpkin patch," Blenda Mushing said. "My friend saw a ghost in your window, too."

"When was that, if you don't mind my asking?" I watched her reaction carefully.

"I don't remember," Blenda said. "I just know it happened."

"If you can't remember, it must have been before Olive Redding took ownership of the house. That would have been while the Sprockets lived there."

"The Sprockets are nice people. If they knew about a ghost, they would have mentioned it today, when—" She stopped suddenly and jerked her thumb at Olive. "Never mind. The ghost came with this one. Everyone knows she has a criminal husband."

"Had," Nigel said. "The criminal husband is past tense."

Blenda gasped. "He's dead? Is he the one in the garden?"

Nigel looked sorry he'd spoken but Keats gave a pant-laugh. Scavenger hunting had become interesting again.

I took over from Nigel. "Ms. Mushing, I happened to see the bones in the yard and they'd been there a very long time." Turning, I found Olive easing toward the door, but Keats didn't need prompting from me to bring her back. Running away from gossip only brought more of it. Better to face it dead on. "Olive, remind me what we need?"

"A candle," she whispered. "Pumpkin spice."

Nigel came over with one. "Smells like those pricey lattes everyone goes nuts over."

I confirmed with a sniff. "Perfect. And now we'll take a piñata. I've got to admit, I'd like to give something a good smack right now. How about you, Nigel?"

He gave me a faint trace of a smile. Progress. "One pumpkin piñata to go, please," he said.

"And the stained glass bat ornament on the shelf behind you," I added.

"Like I said, the last piñata is on hold." Blenda shifted uneasily. "The bat, too. Both for a very good customer." She used her pencil to poke my fingers off the glass display case one by one. "Now, if you'll excuse me, I was in the middle of my accounting."

I put my fingers back, if only to keep her from noticing Keats slipping around the counter and through the curtain. He came back quickly, hackles high, and his blue eye shot me a message.

"We'll take a pumpkin piñata," I repeated. "But if you prefer, I could ask my brother to collect it later. His name is Asher Galloway and he's leading the investigation at Olive's house."

The pencil dropped onto the glass with a clatter. "Is that a threat?"

"Of course not. My brother is just helpful that way. He'll want to go into the back and choose the best piñata. What can I say? The guy has always loved Halloween."

Blenda Mushing put her broom in reverse and slipped through the curtains, pale eyes fixed on mine. "Fine. Take a piñata meant for the sweet kids of Thistledown."

She came back quickly with a pumpkin piñata the size of a basketball and handed it to Nigel. He looked at it with distaste and tucked it under his arm.

"I've already done a lot for Thistledown by clearing a criminal off your streets," I said. "So, I'll take the bat ornament, too, Ms. Mushing."

"You're as unlikable as everyone says, Ivy Galloway." Blenda slapped the bat ornament on the counter hard enough to make a cracking sound.

"The other bat, please. The list says purple and this one is bluish. Again, I could send Asher but he's practically color blind and I could see it taking a while to choose."

Her lips worked soundlessly, but she surrendered the bat. "There's a markup, since I was holding it for a good customer."

"That's fine." I pulled out my credit card. "I'm nothing if not fair."

"Throwing your cop brother's name around is far from fair," Blenda said.

"It's better than throwing my cop fiancé's name around. Either way, why would having a cop visit the store bother you?" I gestured to the plaque on the wall. "You have awards for civic contribution. I can't imagine you're hiding anything nefarious in your piñatas." I glanced at Olive and smiled. "Although, pumpkins are so deceptive. Are they a fruit or a vegetable?"

"Fruit," Olive said, setting a fluffy white spider on the counter. "We'll take this, too, and call it done."

Ms. Mushing handed me a receipt and grumbled insults after us as we left. Keats turned and gave her an impudent yap as the door closed.

On the sidewalk outside, Olive couldn't help smiling and the twinkle lights made her white teeth gleam. "You and Keats are awesome."

Keats gave a brag that wasn't humble at all. "He knows," I said. "But I'll thank you on his behalf, because I'm more likable than some people think."

CHAPTER NINE

I t didn't give me as much satisfaction as I expected to beat Jilly
and Kestra back to the schoolhouse library. Olive continued to
look glum over all that had happened. Kestra looked sad, too.
Perhaps she needed one of the Mafia's dogs to bring her spark back.
Assuming she'd had a spark before. Until I found Keats, I'd unknowingly survived fifteen years without such a spark and with a furry
pilot light now warming my heart, I wanted that for every dog lover.

"That's a worthy goal," Jilly said as I shared my thoughts while
driving through town later that evening. "One I can definitely get
behind. But I'm not sure we can pull it off in the time allowed, especially given the circumstances."

"Maybe not, but hopefully the Reddings will stick around for a
while. Thistledown is just as good a place to transform as Clover
Grove. If the sisters are as decent as they seem, they could have a
readymade community, with Thelma, Maud, Louisa, Wendel
Barrick and the Merriweathers."

"Louisa has become good friends with Zoe Hampton," Jilly said,
bracing Percy and Keats on her lap. "Both pet people, which is the
glue that binds."

I followed the route had Thelma mapped out after showing me a photo in the newspaper records. "With us behind them, there's a good chance both sisters could win a Mafia dog. Whether Olive keeps that house is another matter."

Staring out the passenger window, Jilly shook her head. "Some store had a great deal on plastic skeletons. Glennis Redding was right about seeing them hanging all over town." She turned and looked at me. "I wouldn't keep that house knowing there was a body in the pumpkin patch. Would you?"

I shrugged. "If I liked the place, sure. We're still at Runaway Inn despite a few bodies. Lots of things haunt me, but it isn't those victims. It's the people who killed them."

"Good point. I guess I'd stay if that turned out to be the only thing wrong with the house. While I don't believe there's a ghost, the way Olive's cat behaved made me worry there's another body inside. Did you think about that?"

"I did, yeah. Especially after Kellan mentioned the stack of missing people." I made the last turn out of town and ended up on a road into the countryside. "When the police are done, we'll spend a little time there. Rule out a ghost and find out what's really going on."

"Can I pass on this one?" Her fingers began flying over Percy's fluff. "I'm no ghostbuster, Ivy. Nor even a ghost *story* buster."

After squeezing her arm briefly, I geared down for another, sharper turn. "I know. You're off the hook. Besides, someone needs to cover for me at the event."

"You mean with my husband."

I laughed. "That, too. He's not as trusting as he used to be. You're the only guaranteed distraction."

"As long as it's for a noble cause, I don't mind spending quality time with my husband. Do you know when you're going to need to deploy my wifely wiles?"

"Tonight," I said. "Asher can stay with you in the motel room we booked. I'll crash at Maud's."

Keats had been intent on the road, but he gave a little whine now. He loved visiting his breeder, Maud Gentry, and especially his border collie dam, Annie. His younger sister Frost was more of an annoyance, perhaps as I was to Asher, but they were fond of each other in their own way. Both were highly competitive dogs and spending time with Frost was probably the only thing that truly tired Keats out. His desperate desire to stay ahead of her had given him new skills. In particular, Frost loved scent work and Keats was now training to expert level. Meanwhile, Annie's passion was agility, and while Keats had never been interested when we tried that in his early years he ran Maud's course now with fierce dedication. His drive to keep up with his fur family would benefit both farm work and crime-solving.

"Ivy, you can't go into Olive's house when the investigation's in progress," Jilly reminded me.

"Asher said they'd take a good look around and I'm sure they've done that already. There was no sign of crime inside, according to the pets. I promise I'll stay out of the pumpkin patch." I couldn't hold back a shudder. "Why is a foot so much creepier than a femur?"

"Because it's undeniably human?" Jilly suggested. "But then, you also carried a skull in your purse once."

"A purse I had to throw out. I couldn't even donate it to a good home knowing how it had been used."

"That was the right call, although I believe in donating all the more since I've seen the second life your mom gives clothes." She paused for a moment and then continued. "I just imagined that skull getting a second life. Halloween is doing a number on my own head."

I laughed as I pulled up to a beautifully refurbished red brick farmhouse and parked. The sign out front said Twin Owl Bed and Breakfast, and the decorations were seasonal and tasteful. There were urns full of tall grasses, stacks of white gourds and pots of golden chrysanthemums. As we climbed the stairs I noticed some round, bare patches in the fallen leaves, where pumpkins had likely sat. Perhaps all pumpkins would disappear from Thistledown after the mysterious discovery at Olive's house. Things like this tended to go in the opposite direction, however. Thistledown might well become the pumpkin capital of hill country.

Keats' paw came up before we crossed the stone porch to the door. Percy, meanwhile, skirted a large planter and crouched behind it.

"Uh-oh," Jilly said. "Battle stations."

She smoothed her hair and her coat and then smiled, knowing that her looks and charm were good armor. I did the same, although they had never been quite as reliable for me. The best I could pull off was a solid HR smile.

As the wood door opened, I couldn't help seeing myself through the eyes of the couple staring out at us. Did Jilly and I look like grinning jack-o'-lanterns, albeit the tame and friendly type? I didn't subscribe to the newfangled versions carved from stencils. Some were abstract and others ripped from a horror movie. The point of pumpkin art wasn't to terrify toddlers, at least to my way of thinking.

The screen door framed a middle-aged couple, each with a travel bag slung over one shoulder. The bags jostled together and there wasn't enough room for both to leave at the same time. Both seemed eager to get out.

The movement stopped when they saw us, however, and I thought they were going to go back inside and close the wood door. Someone else poked a hand between them and opened the screen door. "There you go."

When the screen door swung open, the same hand must have propelled them through it because they came out with a lurch. The woman's sensible lace-up shoes seemed to slide across the stone.

"Go along now," a male voice behind them said. "It's always hard to leave our home but you can come back anytime."

Keats gave a ha-ha-ha. The host's tone suggested the opposite, and it was likely his guest book would be too full for subsequent bookings when it came to this couple.

"Hello," Jilly said, in the rich, melodious tone that used to make CEOs crowd at her feet. "You must be the Sprockets."

"Must we?" the man said. It was unclear whether he was being sincere or sarcastic.

"You must." The voice belonged to the host, and he stepped out from behind the couple. He was bald and around seventy, but his smile was youthful, perhaps even impish. "Just as I must be Carsten Towers, host of Twin Owl."

"It looks like we got here just in time," I said. "I have a confession to make to the Sprockets."

Mr. Sprocket stared at me. "It's hardly a big reveal. I know who you are. Everyone does."

That crushed me each time I heard it. It seemed I'd need to go far beyond hill country to escape my reputation. "Well, my confession is a little bigger than just my name. I took your piñata. The big pumpkin Blenda Mushing put aside for you."

Mrs. Sprocket spoke for the first time. "That's okay. We didn't want it anymore anyway."

"Pumpkins aren't as popular around here as they were a day ago," the host said, grinning. "But a room just opened up here if you're looking for accommodation, ladies."

"Thanks, we're covered," Jilly said. "I'm staying with my police officer husband at a motel while he investigates what happened at the Sprockets' home."

"Former home." The couple's voices overlapped, and the man added, "We sold it, fair and square."

"Was it though?" I asked. "A fair sale?"

Mr. Sprocket's scowl might have scared off less intrepid sleuths. "Of course. How could we possibly know there were bones in the garden? Everyone says they're hundreds of years old."

"An exaggeration," I said. "By a century or two."

"Regardless, we only lived there a few years and neither of us has a green thumb." Mrs. Sprocket eyed Keats before adding, "Or much fondness for pets. No offense."

"None taken," I said, over Keats' grumble to the contrary. "If you had pets, you may have been quicker to notice something amiss inside the house."

The man reached for his wife's wrist and squeezed her into silence. "Amiss? The house was lovely. We only left because Thistledown is getting too popular. We like to be surrounded by space and silence."

"Silence," his wife echoed. "Yes. It's so precious these days."

"So, the house was noisy?" I asked. "It's on a quiet street."

The man's fingers must have tightened because Mrs. Sprocket winced. "You could still hear the hustle and bustle of Main Street," he said. "It's as bad as the city."

Jilly tried to muffle a snort and Keats joined her with a pant-laugh.

"What's so funny?" the woman said.

"Just that we lived in Boston for more than a decade," Jilly said. "Thistledown seems quiet to former city slickers like us."

"Maybe the bigger problem was noise *inside* the house," I suggested. "Within the walls, perhaps."

Jilly pointed up at the sky. "Or overhead. That would have been so—"

"Spooky?" Carsten Towers interrupted. "Everyone says the place is haunted. But the town's gone crazy over Halloween. Didn't used to be like this."

"The house is not haunted," Mr. Sprocket said, releasing his wife's wrist to shake his finger at Jilly. "That's ridiculous. We don't believe in such things."

"It was hard to sleep, sometimes." Mrs. Sprocket spoke more freely as she rubbed her wrist. "I just didn't like the house anymore. I love Thistledown, though, and miss it already. We came back for the Halloween rescue event."

"Obviously we wouldn't have come into town if we'd done anything wrong," her husband said. "It's not a crime to decide you want a quieter house."

"Not a crime," I agreed. "But your real estate paperwork said you needed to disclose anything that might cause the buyer emotional distress. And Olive Redding is definitely distressed right now. She can't sleep in the house, either."

"It's not our fault," Mr. Sprocket said. "We did think there might be squirrels in the attic but pest control couldn't find a problem. A contractor sealed up some nooks and crannies."

Keats sat at Mrs. Sprocket's feet and stared as if trying to pull more words out of her with his eerie blue eye. It worked, too. "That's not all we did. Blenda Mushing sold me some sage and I smudged the house. I brought in crystals and even—"

"Honey, stop. That woo-woo talk is going to give them the wrong idea."

"The idea that the house is haunted?" I worked my best HR smile. "What else did Blenda sell you?"

"She came over and did a—a clearing, I think she called it," Mrs. Sprocket said. "An energy clearing. Then she said the evil spirits were gone."

Her husband stared at her. "You never told me that. How much did Blenda charge you?"

"I'd have paid anything to get a good night's sleep by that point. You were out of town and I couldn't take that strange noise."

"Jingling?" I asked.

"Yes!" Her eyes moved from the dog's to mine. "You heard it, too?"

"Hon, you've said too much." Mr. Sprocket reached for her wrist again but his wife evaded his grasp. "Glennis said not to let your imagination run away with you."

Jilly spoke up again. "We don't want to cause trouble. For the new owner's sake, we just want to figure out what's going on at the house."

"Personally, I think it's an animal in need," I added. "That's my area of expertise. Crystals and energy clearings won't help in a situation like that."

"If it really is an animal you won't have to worry about Glennis and Paige Ogilvy," Jilly said. "Ivy will free it. She may even take it home with us to the farm. Just tell her everything you know."

Mr. Sprocket dropped his heavy bag to the stones and surrendered. "It started over two months ago. That noise. We spent over a thousand trying to figure it out and really believed we'd done all we could."

"We certainly never knew about the bones in the garden," his wife said. "Trust me, I'd have been gone a lot sooner."

Keats let me know she was telling the truth. But Percy wasn't fully satisfied. He gave a half sweep with one paw from behind the planter.

"Mrs. Sprocket, what finally drove you out?" I asked.

She stared down at Keats and when Percy leapt to the planter's rim, she stepped backward onto the host's foot. Both gave a little scream, which my pets found entertaining.

"The psychic," she said, at last. "Blenda Mushing sent me to her friend in Dorset Hills who did a tarot card reading."

Her husband rubbed his forehead. "More balderdash I didn't know about."

"The psychic said people died in that house," his wife said. "Just as I suspected."

"People have died in all old houses." Her husband looked at the host. "I bet even here."

Carsten gave his impish smile. "Most definitely. My own grandparents, for starters. They're not jingling around but I wouldn't mind if they did. I was fond of them."

"The psychic was sure bad people died in that house," Mrs. Sprocket said. "Once I knew that, I couldn't stay anymore. It was worth three hundred dollars to know."

"Three hundred? Are you kidding me?" Her husband sighed. "There are charlatans everywhere preying on the sleep deprived. Even today, Blenda was forcing so-called good luck charms on us at her store."

"The pumpkin is supposed to bring wealth," his wife said. "And the bat fends off evil." She smiled at me. "I'm glad you got them. Olive Redding needs them more than we do."

"Maybe not," Carsten said. "Paige Ogilvy is persistent and that house could be back in your hands soon."

Mrs. Sprocket started to cry and Keats withdrew to herd us down the stairs. "That's not in the cards," she said as we left. "The psychic told me so yesterday."

Her husband picked up their bags. "Again? Stop paying these scammers."

"You can't put a price tag on sanity," his wife said. "I'd like you to see her, too."

They followed us down to their car and he grumbled as he opened the trunk. "Let's go back to the country. It's easier to be sane there."

"Really?" Jilly muttered, climbing into the truck.

"Not really," I said, joining her. "It's hard to be sane anywhere. Especially at Halloween."

CHAPTER TEN

I left my friends with the Redding sisters at the motel that evening, telling them I was heading to Maud Gentry's house. Eventually that would be true. The breeder had given me permission to arrive whenever I finished my ghost hunting.

After parking at the library, I walked the rest of the way to Olive's place with Keats and Percy. Then I settled in some bushes in front of the house to wait out Officer Wiebe. The young keener lingered for ages, probably hoping for his big break in the case.

Luckily, the go-kit Edna constantly restocked with seasonally appropriate gear contained a lightweight waterproof blanket that blocked the chill from the cold earth. How could we be heading into winter again so soon? It barely felt like the last one was over. Maybe that's how every year would feel now that I was happy with my life. When I was an HR exec, every day, every month, every season dragged on interminably. The misery crept up so gradually I didn't realize it until I'd nearly suffocated.

Keats bonked me in the nose with his muzzle. "Hey," I whispered. "What was that for? I wasn't falling asleep or anything. How could I when there's so much adrenaline in my veins?"

Many a time Keats had prevented me from doing just that, but tonight he was probably prodding me out of rumination. He had little patience for that lately. So little I might have gotten a nip, except he didn't want me to scream.

Finally, Officer Wiebe drove away, trolling slowly along the road. I suspected he'd be back during the night, but hopefully he'd take a few hours to rest. I really needed to hang out in the house for a while if I hoped to get to the bottom of this issue.

I wouldn't be alone the whole time. A pair of good friends were meeting us here. In fact, Percy's bristling told me they were already in the vicinity. While I was still folding the blanket, a woman walked around the side of the house to the back door. I knew who it was because she was wearing a dress and heels. There were only two people of my acquaintance who'd risk stilettos in loose, damp earth and my mother was safely under the watchful eyes of my sisters at Runaway Inn.

Keats agreed with a mumble and then poked me to hurry. Meanwhile, Percy ran ahead. A few moments later, an eerie howl told me he was menacing Olive's cat through the glass again. She hadn't been able to find Cinders to take her to the motel, but we'd promised to come back with reinforcements.

When I came around the house, the woman was standing beside the excavated garden. I flicked on my phone briefly and saw a face similar to that of my best friend. Their green eyes were virtually identical, but this woman's abundant curls were dark. It was Jilly's cousin, Janelle Brighton. Tucked under one arm was her dachshund, Mr. Bixby.

"Let's talk inside," she said. "The door's unlocked."

I didn't know how she opened it, nor did I ask. Janelle was quite capable of jimmying a lock and had skills that defied imagination. Some she'd gained from working her way up from maintenance roles at hotels and resorts. Others were inborn and better not discussed if I wanted to stay on Jilly's good side. The cousins had been extremely close as children, fallen out as teens, and were in a good place again

—at least as long as Janelle avoided openly discussing her intangible gifts. That may have frustrated Janelle at one time, but now I sensed only relief.

We had become adept at talking around what appeared to be supernatural abilities. From what I had witnessed, Janelle truly was a psychic, or at least extremely gifted at reading a situation. It didn't bother me that she believed she could see and hear ghosts, and it didn't bother me that I couldn't. Sometimes, it felt like I was on the verge of crossing that divide, but I either fell back, or was shoved back, and it was just as well. There was enough going on in my life without throwing magic in the mix.

Still, I was always curious and had to stop myself from asking too much. Not for myself, but for Jilly. She had been traumatized in her early life by her family's belief in such things and wanted to stick with what she could see and touch and experience in this realm. After all we'd been through together, I owed it to her to respect her feelings around this, so we'd adopted a "don't ask, don't tell" policy. My best friend may have suspected I'd call on Janelle tonight because the hug she gave me as I left the motel seemed a little extra— enough to share with someone else. So I did that now, squishing the dachshund only slightly and not hard enough to deserve the indignant complaints he sent my way.

"Sorry, Mr. Bixby," I said, pulling away. "My aim's a little off in the dark."

Janelle pulled a flashlight out of her purse and turned it on. "Don't worry, no one will see this."

I took her at her word. There was a lot of space between houses, and she may have sensed Officer Wiebe was far out of range. On the other hand, there could be something special about that flashlight. This was another case of "don't ask, don't tell." Either way, I valued that light. Even with Janelle's impressive confidence, I was uneasy here.

"Is it haunted?" I asked, as she paused in the front hall. "Can you tell?"

"Give me a minute. It's not like I can just stick a thermometer into a house and tell if it's cooked." She grinned over her shoulder. "As convenient as that would be. I'd love to patent such a gizmo. I'd be one rich..." The dog interjected a yip and she finished "woman."

Janelle's heels clicked over the hardwood as she led me around the main floor of the house. She muttered very quietly under her breath. It didn't sound like an incantation—just a regular one-sided conversation like I had with Keats every day. I suspected that's exactly what was going on, and the only difference between us was that she hid it better.

Well, maybe not the only difference. When both Janelle and Mr. Bixby cocked their heads at precisely the same moment, and the dachshund gave an audible and very expressive grumble, I sensed a clear exchange of information. Janelle's laugh seemed to confirm it.

"What?" I asked. "What did I just miss?"

She turned and her teeth gleamed in the flashlight's glow. "Just Bixby being Bixby. He thinks I brought him here under false pretenses."

"No ghost?"

The dachshund grumbled in an irritable tone. Though his vocalization was similar enough to Keats' mumbles, I couldn't understand him at all. It was a totally different language.

"I don't sense a ghost," Janelle said. "Although there was a lot of unhappiness in this home. Recently and long ago. Also duplicity and greed. Those emotions leave an imprint."

I nodded. "Even I can feel that and I'm no psychic." Mr. Bixby almost seemed to chuckle and I added, "Well, I'm not. Jilly would kill me."

"Ignore my cheeky darling. Anyway, he's come to a more mundane conclusion about what's happening here."

"Pests?" I asked.

"Apparently. And while this pedigreed dachshund is bred to hunt, he mostly doesn't bother getting his paws dirty anymore."

"Hunt what, in this case?"

"Something so small it's beneath his notice."

I stared at the dachshund, who was examining his claws with more interest than the room. "Like a mouse?"

He glanced up at me with expressive brown eyes and yawned.

"Come now, Bixby," Janelle said. "This is important to Ivy, and therefore important to us."

"If it's a mouse, why hasn't it succumbed to multiple exterminators? Or the new owner's cat?" I glanced at Percy, who was heading up the stairs. "Percy is like Bixby... he doesn't hunt small prey anymore."

The dachshund bristled a bit, perhaps objecting to being compared to a cat. Or any other creature. He was in a class unto himself, at least in his own mind.

The sleek dog's ears flopped fetchingly as he stared at me and I couldn't help smiling. Janelle met my eyes and smiled, too, while giving her dog a little squeeze. "I'm not picking up ghosts and he's not picking up squirrels, possums or raccoons. Those usually do get a bigger reaction than a yawn. That pretty much leaves a mouse."

"But how on earth could a mouse create a din that terrifies owners? And evade so many who want him gone?"

"Her," Janelle said. "Don't quote me on that, but I'm picking up a lot of feminine vibes around here."

"Any idea where? It could take time to find a small mouse in a big house, when she's clearly elusive."

Janelle beckoned and then followed Percy up the stairs. "She may be elusive with exterminators, but you do have a way about you, Ivy. I bet you can sweet talk her out of hiding, but it won't be till Bixby is gone. This mouse may be beneath his notice, but he won't be beneath hers." Her dog grumbled and she added, "That wasn't a slight about your height, my friend."

"There are two cats here, and I'm sure a mouse would consider Keats a threat."

She shone her light around. "If the resident cat was an issue, the mouse would be gone by now. And your pets are trained to accept all creatures great and small. Except homicidal maniacs."

"Just the same, I worry. What if I lure this mouse out and—"

A sharp, short shriek from Janelle cut me off.

"Sorry, Bixby," she said. "Sorry Keats and Percy. It's just—"

"The doll. I know. So creepy."

"And obviously I'm not easily creeped out. But there's something off about that thing. I'd almost say it's hexed."

"Hexed! Do you think?"

She examined it from every angle, and Bixby deigned to stick his nose out for a good sniff, too. "Not hexed. Just properly creepy. Probably comes with a past."

"Can you take it away?" I asked. "I'm afraid to touch it."

"I'm not touching it, either. If a house carries spiritual residue, so can an antique. But it's probably harmless." She paused as Bixby mumbled. "Perhaps more harmless than others would like. I suspect it was left here for the very reason of unsettling people."

"Mission accomplished." My eyes followed the beam of light as she directed it around the room. "Is this the mouse's secret lair?"

Shaking her head, Janelle turned and walked down the hall to the master bedroom at the front of the house. "More like here. I think the mouse wanted to be as far away from the pumpkin patch as possible."

"Makes sense. I'm happier away from that, too." I dropped my pack in a corner. "Maybe if I just settle in for a bit, she'll come out and tell me her story."

"Good plan. You know animals better than I do." She went to the front window, where light came in from the street, and then turned off her own. "What I can tell you is that you probably have a couple of hours before that young officer comes back."

I let out a sigh of relief. "That's a huge help, thanks. I can relax and wait. Or at least wait."

She laughed. "There's probably not much relaxation here but at least you know there's no ghost. Nothing I can detect, anyway. My experience isn't vast."

Pulling out the blanket again, I spread it on the floor. "I trust you. Are you going to stick around for a bit?"

"Wish I could but we've got a situation in Wyldwood Springs. What else is new?"

"Plus you're afraid Asher will come by and tell Jilly you were here," I said.

She laughed again as she walked out of the room. "Yeah. I'm more afraid of Jilly than the situation in Wyldwood. I won't lie."

"Janelle, wait."

Turning at the door, she cocked her head in unison with Mr. Bixby again. The way her curls and his ears flopped was remarkably similar. They were both so attractive, although perhaps she wouldn't find the comparison flattering.

Her smile expanded, making me wonder if she'd picked up on that thought. "What is it?" she asked.

"The body from the pumpkin patch. Do you have any idea who it might be? Or if there are more people unceremoniously dumped on this property?"

She closed her eyes and took a deep breath. "I don't think so? And yes, that was a question mark. I don't sense a spirit in this house but nothing is ever certain outdoors, at least for me."

I sighed. "I figured that would be too easy."

"Don't worry. You've got this."

Keats mumbled assurance that we did, although he didn't sound as enthused about it as usual. Maybe he didn't like being left with a case beneath Bixby's notice.

"I'm not that big on mice," I said as she left. "And I hate Halloween."

"You and me both, my friend."

"Just stay a little longer," I called after her, but she was already hurrying down the hall. A few moments later, laughter floated up the stairs.

"She sounds just like Jilly," I muttered to the boys.

"Don't tell her that, Ivy," she called, although she couldn't possibly have heard me—and I shouldn't have been able to hear her that well, either. "And beware of—"

Why did that last word have to be the only one I couldn't pick up? And why did it sound so similar to "rats?"

CHAPTER ELEVEN

Propping myself against a wall with a pet on either side, I prepared for a long wait in the empty bedroom. Olive had set up her bed in the middle room, probably because it was quiet. There was so little furniture in the house, I sensed she'd been ready to pull up stakes from the start.

Maybe I dozed for a bit because it didn't seem like much time had passed before I heard a strange sound.

Olive and the house's previous owner had described it as a jingle but that wasn't quite how it struck me. There was a clinking, metallic quality to it, but it wasn't musical at all. In fact, it was utterly doleful.

"Stay," I told the dog and cat, holding their collars, just to be safe. "This is our big break."

The big break, as it turned out, was actually a very small break in the cupboard door. Releasing the dog, I turned on my phone light and sent its beam in the direction of the sound. Two bright and beady eyes peered out at me from under the crack. When I didn't move, the mouse forced its way out but then it just stood there. I gave the creature time, assuming it was taking stock of a potentially treacherous situation.

Then its little paws scrabbled on the floor, as if it was trying unsuccessfully to come toward me.

Something was holding it back. It gave what appeared to be a mighty tug for a mouse and then flattened, perhaps exhausted by the effort.

"What's going on, my tiny friend?" I asked. "Do you need some help?"

The mouse's eyes stayed on me, but it didn't move.

"Oh gosh, I'm a little out of my league here." Releasing the dog's collar, I said, "Keats, stay. And keep Percy here, too." I waggled my fingers in front of the cat's fixed stare. "Percy, do not even think about it. You're a superhero, not a barn cat. And I give Keats permission to remind you of that if needed. Understood?"

Neither pet made a sound. Their ears came forward, but that was it.

"All right. I'm going in."

Shifting to my hands and knees, I lowered myself till I was flat on my belly and inched toward the mouse. Never had I been more acutely aware of my size or distinct lack of grace. To that mouse, I must seem like a big, clumsy oaf.

It wasn't long before my light picked up the problem, however.

The mouse was very clearly stuck. A faint glimmer behind her suggested a silver or gold chain had snagged her back paw. Or perhaps her tail.

"Oh, no! That must be very heavy for a wee thing like you."

The mouse let me creep up, inch by inch, till we were merely a foot apart. She was far prettier than I expected, with brown hair in shades of rust and brown that contrasted nicely with her white underbelly. Her nose and white whiskers twitched comically, and delicate round ears rose and flattened as she took in the new situation. It seemed like her bright eyes sparkled with intelligence.

Keats mumbled behind me, as if to suggest I was too easily

impressed. When it came to animals, that was probably true. Not so much humans.

Setting the phone down, I reached into the front pocket of my overalls and pulled out my new multitool. There was a little hook on it I hadn't used before that might suit this very occasion. Maybe it was meant for mouse fishing.

I reached around the mouse, snagged the chain and pulled gently. The fine links emerged from the crack bit by bit before ultimately lodging there.

"What's holding it?" I eased closer still. Holding the chain with one finger so that it wouldn't jerk the mouse around, I pulled harder with my tool. It took some finessing but finally I saw the edge of what appeared to be a piece of jewelry. A watch, perhaps.

"Sorry, Millicent," I whispered. "Millicent the Magnificent. Never Millie. I'm going to have to crack the door open to release you. Can you scoot along a little?"

I reached over my head and twisted the handle until the door was ajar. The mouse got the general idea, moving toward the opening and letting me drag the chain behind her with my hook. When she reached the gap, a circular object slid into view.

It wasn't a watch, but an old locket.

"Uh-oh, boys. It looks like her foot is trapped in the clasp. She'll never be able to take care of herself while she's dragging that around. In fact, she might already be injured. I'll need to get it off."

Keats mumbled something like, "Good luck with that."

"Unhelpful, sir. Unhelpful. This would be difficult in daytime with bright light and a magnifying glass. What if she bites?"

His next mumble was nicer.

"Good point. I suppose she must want to be helped, and by me in particular. No one else has seen her."

Sitting up, I crossed my legs and settled in for a think. There was a real risk of my harming the mouse by pulling the chain off her foot. A mouse without four working paws was a mouse who wouldn't last long. Likely the only reason she'd avoided traps set out by extermina-tors was accessibility. She couldn't go far dragging a locket around.

I flipped through the various options on the multitool. Thank goodness I had it, because the pliers in my pocket were bigger than the actual mouse.

"Tweezers! If I use my flashlight plus the phone camera to magnify her foot, I could probably ease the chain off. But she'd need to cooperate and I don't see why she would."

Keats gave Percy a poke with his nose and the cat followed him into the hall.

"Good idea," I said. "She's more likely to let me try if she doesn't have furry predators watching. But don't go far." I stared up at the window, looking for headlights. "We may not have as long as Janelle predicted."

After the dog and cat left to explore, I crawled over to my back-pack and pulled it with me to the closet. Spreading the blanket on the floor, I stretched out on top of it and then propped my phone against the pack. It took a few minutes to set up my flashlight and camera but eventually I had the mouse in a circle of light. She looked almost like an illustration from a children's book. A mouse performer preparing to deliver a soliloquy, sing an aria or bust some dance moves.

"This is a story I'll tell my kids someday," I said. "Leaving out the part about the skeleton in the pumpkin patch."

The procedure only took about five minutes in total, but I had to stop twice because I was holding my breath and getting light-headed. My fear of blowing Millicent across the room was undermining my progress.

In the end, the mouse basically took over. While I held the clasp steady with my tweezers, she twisted one way and then the other until she found an angle that allowed her paw to come loose.

Again, I held my breath as I waited for her to move away. Was she injured? From what the former homeowners said, I had to assume the mouse was dragging the locket and chain for more than a month. Her fur was surprisingly lush, considering. Perhaps if she'd been living in the attic, other rodents had stored nuts there. I'd seen oak, beech, black walnut and chestnut trees in the neighborhood, along with industrious squirrels. Any house this old would have gaps in the eaves, even with a diligent contractor trying to fill them.

The mouse did a full turn, nose up, whiskers twitching. Her cute round ears flattened against her head and she let out a piercing squeak that brought Keats and Percy back at a run.

"What? What?" I asked.

Keats lifted his paw and I saw headlights outside.

I switched off my own lights. "Officer Wiebe's back."

Keats' hackles came up and Percy puffed to echo the sentiment.

"Into the closet. All of us. Step lightly, boys. Do not trample Millicent."

I needn't have worried about the mouse. Her back paw was working well enough to get a grip on my jacket cuff and then shoot up my sleeve. After circling my arm a couple of times and pausing in my armpit, she ascended to my shoulder—Percy's typical perch.

It wasn't ideal, but at least I knew where she was and could avoid squishing her. Grabbing the backpack, blanket and locket, I motioned the boys inside. "After you."

The closet was so deep I began to wonder if we'd find a row of fur coats and then a portal into Narnia, but except for an old wooden ladder hanging from hooks on the wall, it was empty. If Jacob Wiebe happened to look in here, he would get quite a surprise.

I blocked the crack under the door with the blanket and turned on the flashlight. At floor level, this was just your typical old closet, but when I shone the light up, I gasped. The trapdoor to the attic was open a few inches and a black object hung from the ledge. Make that six objects.

Bats.

Could they be fake? More of the Halloween decorations adorning the town?

One of the critters stretched its wings and settled again.

Not fake.

"Why are you here?" I asked. "It's nighttime. Shouldn't you be out catching the last of the mosquitos?"

I had nothing against bats, in general. They had a niche like every other creature and I considered them an important part of the ecosystem at Runaway Farm. But the idea of being trapped in a closet with a half dozen of them was another matter entirely. What if they dropped and got stuck in my hair? Hopefully that was an urban myth, too. Just in case, I tucked my ponytail into the back of my jacket.

"Focus," I told myself. If there was one command I heard more than any other in my life, it was that word. So simple, yet so challenging for someone slowly recovering from a head injury. I was sitting in a closet with a mouse working her way inside my T-shirt, a half dozen bats hanging overhead and a cop coming into the house after me. There would be much to explain to my brother later.

In the meantime, however, I could focus on one thing, and decided to make that the locket clasped so tightly in my palm it left a circular groove. I would likely need to surrender it soon.

Setting the light on the floor, I pried at the edges of the locket until it opened stiffly. Inside was a photograph of a woman. Although the black-and-white image had faded and curled, the face looking back at me was attractive, if severe. It seemed like no one ever smiled in those old photos. Pulling out the same pick I'd used to drag the locket earlier, I gently pried out the photo. Behind it was another photo of a young man whose mustache threatened to swallow his face. On the opposite side of the locket, swirling letters intertwined. It looked like the initials "E" and "O."

I took a few photos and then a paw landed on my leg. The message was the same as I'd given myself a minute ago. *Focus*. Only this time it wasn't on the locket or even the bats overhead, but the front door creaking open downstairs.

Dropping the necklace in my pocket, I pulled the blanket up over us and turned out my light.

Footsteps squeaked over the hardwood in the living and dining rooms and then started up the stairs.

I had my right hand on Keats' head, my left on Percy's back and we stayed perfectly still. The mouse also became motionless, too light to be detectable but for the slight prick of her claws on my skin.

My heart pounded harder, making it difficult to hear footsteps. Keats' muzzle swiveled, however, letting me know the visitor's whereabouts. Unfortunately, that visitor appeared to be in the bedroom with us and coming to the closet door.

Percy was the first to go to high alert, and fluff swallowed my fingertips. There was a nearly-inaudible rumble in Keats' throat. Nothing that a visitor would notice.

The dog moved into a crouch, and that alarmed me more than anything. It meant he was prepared to rocket into the face of whoever opened the door, whereas, to my knowledge, we were under no threat. I expected nothing worse than a verbal beatdown from my brother, followed by another from my fiancé. Young Officer Wiebe hardly warranted such a reaction.

Unless there was something I was missing...

Keats rumbled again, this time a reply. There was definitely something I was missing. Maybe it wasn't Officer Wiebe at all.

I eased the blanket down, in case the pets did indeed need to launch.

The dog's head swiveled back again, faster, as if the person were making an exit—and a swift one. Percy deflated quickly and my breath evened out. I wasn't going anywhere until the boys told me the coast was clear, but I was comfortable now. Or at least as comfortable as one could be with a rodent on one's shoulder and winged critters hanging overhead. As my panic subsided, I heard the rustle of wings. Then a tiny squeak came from inside my clothing. I didn't speak mouse but it sounded animated. Perky. I guess after being on the chain gang, her current accommodation was a pleasant enough change. At least she was warm.

"Are we good?" I whispered. "I've had enough excitement for one night."

Keats' head swiveled again and this time, I not only heard boots, but felt the vibration under me. Either someone new had arrived or the original visitor was feeling more assertive. The dog dropped to a pounce position again, only this time it felt different.

This time he was most definitely going to launch.

And I wasn't going to be able to stop him.

CHAPTER TWELVE

The door opened and flooded the closet with so much light my eyeballs nearly exploded. I let go of Keats' collar to shield my face and felt the whoosh of air and fur as he leapt. Percy did the same on my other side, leaving me scrambling to untangle myself from the blanket and get my limbs organized.

A man yelped and the boots clomped backward.

Any other man may have full-on screamed, including my brother. But this man... this man had been ambushed so often that even in a supposedly empty and haunted house, he was somewhat prepared for a ploy like this. The dog and cat had trained him so well they'd spoiled their own fun.

"Stop it, you two," he said "Leave my uniform alone. John Keats Galloway, if my bootlaces are snipped, I'll toss you in lockup with the other canine riffraff."

"Leave it, boys," I said.

I stopped trying to free myself and grinned just as the light hit me again.

"Hey. Hey! HEY!"

Now it was a proper scream. He dropped the light and it spun in circles, creating a strobe effect.

"What's wrong?" I managed to flip onto my hands and knees. "Kellan, what's happening?"

"Birds! They're divebombing me."

"Oh, that. It's not birds, it's bats."

"Bats!" His voice took on a shrill note I hadn't heard before. "Are you serious?"

"Absolutely. I was shut in the closet with them and they were good as gold. Seems like you got them worked up. Guess they don't like cops."

"Cops don't like bats, either. Ivy, call them off."

"I'm not the boss of the bats, Kellan. I'm not even boss of my own pets."

Keats gave a ha-ha-ha, although he'd retreated to the far side of the room. He wasn't big on bats either, it seemed. Percy, on the other hand, was crouched at Kellan's feet, mesmerized. If my fiancé didn't move, the cat was going to—

"Ow! Percy, get down. You are not going to hunt bats from my shoulder."

"He's not going to hunt bats at all," I said. "We're on their turf."

"A master bedroom is not bat turf, last time I checked." He glared at me. "Don't get any big ideas about adding some to the farm interior design."

The cat settled for Kellan's midriff, hooking onto his belt with three paws and swiping at the bats with another. His paws were nowhere in range, but I doubted he really cared to catch them. Percy always enjoyed being at the center of a circus. Kellan, not so much.

I came out of the closet and waved the blanket around gently. "Shoo, bats. Up and out, all of you. Go add some drama to the Halloween festivities."

Surprisingly, they retreated, vanishing one by one into the closet.

"Thank goodness," Kellan said. "I don't know what we would have done."

"I do. It wouldn't have been my first live bat capture and release but it's always a bit of a hassle."

He bent to pick up his light, perhaps deliberately squishing Percy. The cat dropped to the floor with a disgruntled meow and followed the bats into the closet.

When Kellan straightened, he was the chief again. "Would you mind explaining why you were hiding in the closet at the site of a crime scene?"

"The crime scene was out back and decades ago," I said. "The only crime in here is tall tales about haunting. I came to see if there was any truth to the rumors."

"And you brought in Janelle Brighton for a private consult?"

I stared at him. "Did you put a camera on the place?"

"Not me. Officer Wiebe. He's the local cop and gets to do things his way. But knowing that, I figured I'd come down and make sure you didn't do anything crazy. About an hour too late, apparently."

"I didn't do anything crazy. Or not too crazy. After Janelle left, I just sat in the bedroom for a while, soaking in the ambience."

"Soaking? Okay. And then you climbed into the closet, because...?"

"Because I saw headlights. I figured it was Officer Wiebe and I'd get a lecture. But it was you and I'm getting a bigger lecture."

He leaned against a wall and sighed. "That's the thing. It wasn't me, at least at first. Someone came in through the back door and left in a hurry."

I stiffened. "Really? That explains why Keats and Percy got so riled at first. Did the camera catch who it was?"

He shook his head. "Hoodie. Balaclava. Average size. Could be either gender, but I'll take a closer look at the footage."

"Why would someone be creeping around here?"

"Said the creeper to the cop."

"I wasn't creeping. I have permission from the owner to be here. Am I wearing a balaclava? No, I am not."

"But you were lurking in a closet under a blanket. Like a creeper."

"Only because I thought Jacob might be too scared to look in there and I could hide from the lecture."

"Well?" Finally, Kellan smiled at me. "After soaking it all in... what did you find?"

"What makes you think I found anything?"

He tipped his head, evaluating me. "I don't know. Your posture? You're hiding something. I'm sure of it."

I certainly was, and I didn't think he'd care to hear about the mouse circling my midriff under my T-shirt. There's only so much the sexiest man in the world could find appealing in his lady, and that probably didn't include rodent droppings. Or fleas. I was pretty sure rats and mice could host fleas even at this time of year. Keats and Percy were treated, but I wasn't. The thought made me twitch more than the little paws. Either Millicent was busy looking for a way out or she was enjoying her freedom and new terrain to explore.

"I found a mouse," I said. "More specifically, she found me."

"A mouse? I heard the realtors were practically lobbing exterminators at each other."

"And yet Millicent escaped them all."

The flashlight's beam rose and wobbled as he rubbed his forehead. "The mouse has a name? That worries me, Ivy. When you name animals, they seem to step into the spotlight."

"That's exactly what Millicent did. When I shone my light on her it was like she became the star in her own production. I'm just the stagehand."

He quirked one eyebrow. I wasn't aware that Kellan had mastered the independent eyebrow maneuver. It reminded me of his hardware store mentor, Thirl Norland. They had been spending more time together. "And what's the production? Of Mice and Men?"

"Of Mice and Women, I think. Millicent brought me a locket."

He slumped a little against the wall. "The mouse? How on earth could she bring you a locket?"

"It wasn't easy. The poor thing has probably been dragging it for ages. That's why Olive and the previous owners said they heard jingling."

I thought he would stick to the main conversational highway, but the bats hadn't thrown him off his game that much because he took the fork in the road. The dangerous one, at least for me. "You talked to the previous owners?"

"They were in town, so I wanted to know what they knew."

"About the body in the pumpkin patch?"

"No, although I would have been interested in hearing anything about that. Mainly I wanted to know if this so-called haunting involved a trapped animal. Like Olive, the Sprockets had heard jingling. So that ultimately led me to Millicent. I figured I'd solved the mystery of the haunted house, but hearing of this intruder, I wonder if there's more going on here than we know."

"Ivy. There was a body in the garden. There's something going on, which means you don't go poking around. Especially outside my jurisdiction."

"If Asher's running lead, it's still your jurisdiction."

"And yet it's not."

"But it's an old crime. Very old."

"Maybe there's more to it. You know how twisted these things get. One day your pets are digging up a foot and the next, you're in a car chase. It's best to assume that all crimes lead to trouble and try to keep your nose clean." His light ran over me. "You're a little dusty."

"I was lying on the floor earlier. I had to extract the mouse's paw from the locket."

"Of course you did." His tone had the exasperated note of a man who'd heard many outlandish things from his lady love, yet still adored her.

"Well, Millicent showed herself only to me, Kellan. She wanted my help and I gave it to her. In return, I got this. For the police."

I pulled the locket out of my pocket and handed it to him. Dangling it from his fingertips, he said, "You're assuming it has significance?"

"Well, yeah." Now my tone had the exasperated note. "It's old. Ergo, it likely relates to the pumpkin patch situation. Inside you'll find a couple of faces. I'm going to guess one of them owned that foot."

He stared at me, weighing a decision. "There were four."

"Four what?"

"Four feet. Two bodies in the same grave."

I found my own wall to lean against, being careful to locate the mouse's location first. "Seriously? No wonder Percy got so wound up." I waved at the locket. "That's them. Once young and in love and now fertilizer for classic symbols of the Halloween season."

Prying open the locket, he glanced inside. "We can't make a conclusion."

"A mouse dragged that locket to me, Kellan. I've got to assume there's a reason."

He shifted it from one palm to the other, as if mentally weighing it. "Was this a giant mouse? Like a... you-know-what?"

"Just your average mouse. Maybe cuter. Rats can weigh a pound so pulling a locket around wouldn't be hard. It was a champion move for Millicent."

Dropping the locket into a plastic bag, he kept his eyes on me. "And where is she now? This Millicent. Is she available to give a statement?"

"I believe she is, yes. I could put in a good word for you."

He came across the room but stopped a couple of feet from me. "I'd direct your remarks to your left shoulder. If your squirming is any indication, she's headed in that direction."

"Hmmm. Well, I guess your chief voice intimidated her."

"Ivy, please tell me you're not going to wander around with a mouse in your shirt. People already talk about the dog and the cat."

"And plenty more. But no, that's not the plan. Until tonight I didn't know about Millicent the Magnificent, so I didn't bring a cage." The mouse stopped moving and dug in her claws, making me add, "She's a wild mouse. Doesn't belong in a cage."

"Or under a shirt," he pointed out.

"True enough. I'll check in with her about her plans. I think she's just giddy to have her mobility back."

"I suppose knowing a mouse is behind the spooky sounds will ease Olive's mind about the house?"

"Maybe, but I can't imagine she'll want to keep this place when she hears there were four feet in the garden. Murder was listed with haunting in the real estate clause about emotional harm."

"You'll have plenty of time to inquire while you're helping her win a dog in the rescue event," he said. "What's on for tomorrow?"

"Fall fair, corn maze, costume party auction and haunted house." I held up my hand. "Not this house. Cori got a better offer."

"That should be enough activity to keep you out of trouble."

"Definitely." A piercing squeak from my shoulder suggested otherwise, but luckily Kellan didn't speak mouse. I was just learning, but I knew this critter had plenty to tell me, and as always I was willing to listen.

"Ivy?" Kellan asked. "I'll see you out, but maybe I'll skip the hug tonight."

"I don't blame you. I'm hoping Millicent decides to stay behind with her bat friends."

Kellan shook his head. "She won't. Because you're not allowed to visit until Asher and I say so. And this mouse wants your ear."

Millicent popped out of my collar on cue and reached up to grab one of the dangling pearl earrings my generous fiancé had given me for my birthday. I think he intended them for special occasions but there were so few of those in the life of the hobby farmer that I decided to take Jilly's advice and wear them every day. Whether my hair was up, down or anywhere in between, I felt good knowing I had my pearls.

I gently tugged the pearl out of her paws. "Sorry, girl. I'd give you the shirt off my back, but not my earrings. Those are special."

"Thank you for that," Kellan said. "Looks like she has a thing for jewelry. Isn't that a bit odd for a mouse?"

"I would think." Letting Millicent hop onto my hand, I bent and tried to offload her. I didn't want to be transporting a mouse around Thistledown for any number of reasons. For starters, one wrong move could so easily injure her.

Instead of jumping off, however, the lively mouse poked her head into my sleeve and disappeared with a flurry of claws.

Keats gave a rumble of disapproval that Kellan echoed. On this, the most important males in my life were in full agreement.

"Millicent, please," I said. "It's not safe for you to be traveling with me. In case you haven't noticed, one of my ride-or-die friends is a cat."

Percy climbed onto Kellan's shoulder and looked resolutely away. It was less about respect for the mouse than revulsion. He had put up with a lot during our adventures but apparently he was ready to draw the line here.

"I'm sorry, Percy," I said. "Millicent has made her decision. If you want to stay with Jilly at the motel, Kellan can drop you off."

"I'm not a cat shuttle." Kellan sounded slightly miffed. "But I suppose I could make an exception for this."

Percy turned, held out one paw to me and flexed his claws. I collected him from Kellan's shoulder. "Okay, then. Best behavior, please."

Kellan brushed the fur off his coat. "I thought he was going to pass."

I got Percy settled into the crook of my arm. By this point, I had no idea where Millicent was situated but she was going to have to keep her wits about her. "Maybe Percy thinks there's more work ahead for him. No matter how much the current situation disgusts him, he won't neglect his duty. This cat is a professional."

The long groan that escaped Kellan's lips made me smile. "A professional *what?*"

"Detector of bodies, among other things."

My beloved layered another groan on top of the first. "More bodies?"

The cat lolled on his back in my arms and then gave a casual sweep of both paws. Just a one-two. Claws splayed. "That's what I'm picking up." Standing on tiptoe, I kissed Kellan's cheek. "So glad you came down."

CHAPTER THIRTEEN

Thelma pulled up in her Land Rover and parked beside the truck outside the library. Both of us had the sense to stay well away from Cori's boobytrapped fake body. I'd already had my share of scares for today.

"This had better be important, Ivy," the librarian said, climbing out of her vehicle. "I was watching my show."

She was wearing a gold velour tracksuit that dated back a few decades and a silk turban over her curls. I had probably gotten her out of bed, or at least her recliner, if she had one. I couldn't imagine Thelma using a recliner, but then I wouldn't have imagined her in a tracksuit, either. I pegged her for a prim flannel nightshirt, matching robe and slippers with a sensible rubber sole. Instead, she was in tan suede clogs with a platform sole.

"What's your show?" I asked, letting Keats herd her up the ramp to the front door.

She eyed me over her glasses while sticking a key in the lock. It was so routine she didn't need to look. "Any reality show competition is my show. And I'll thank you not to judge. A historian who spends so much time with her head in the past needs something like that to ground her in the present."

"Got it." I followed her inside. "But I need to take you back into the past tonight."

"The treasure map?" she asked.

I shook my head. "I don't think so. Doesn't seem as old as pirate's gold or other ill-gotten booty. It's just a pretty locket, now in the possession of my fiancé."

She motioned for me to walk with her to the back room. "I suppose Kellan came down to figure out who owned the foot in the Redding yard?"

"Feet. Plural."

Her clogs, thumping on the industrial carpet, slowed as she pondered my meaning. "How many exactly? Was it a mass killing?"

"Just four feet, to my knowledge. Although Kellan doesn't always disclose the full story."

"Can you blame the man?" She unlocked the door to her office, also quite automatically. "You're likely to go off and run a parallel investigation. I assume that's what we're doing?"

"I gave him the evidence, and you can share any intel with him when he shows up."

"He wouldn't have the audacity to pull me off my Victorian fainting couch after a long day." She glared at me. "I wish everyone showed that respect."

I countered her glare with a grin. "Thelma, your brave sacrifice will give you bragging rights. You're getting to see what I found at the Redding house before Dottie. Before Edna. Before the home-owner. Before Jilly, even. Only Kellan knows what I found. And now, you."

Her expression softened under the turban. At first, I thought the fabric was black, but it was deep bronze, with flecks of gold. I wondered if her fainting couch matched the ensemble, too.

"That does make a difference." She made sure the pets were clear of the door and then locked it behind us. "What did you find?"

I pulled out my phone. "Kellan kept the real thing, unfortunately, but I have photos."

She shoved her glasses back up and angled my phone toward the light, flipping quickly. "Uh-huh. Ah, yes. Oh, my."

I accepted the phone back. "Care to elaborate?"

"I'll go one better." Walking to her desk, she booted up the computer. "I suppose we could go out into the library and comb the collection in the old-fashioned way, but there's a time and place for technology and that's when I'm missing my show."

She thrummed her fingers on her desk as she waited and then, with a few clicks, called up the archives of the Thistledown newspaper. It had been defunct for some years now but used to be a strong weekly. I missed the newspapers of my youth. The few that survived weren't very reliable. Perhaps they never were, but back in the day, they seemed more impartial. Justine Schalow's new incarnation of the *Clover Grove Tattler* was the worst example of shady reporting.

Finally, Thelma turned the monitor with a flourish to show me a photograph. "It's them!" I said. "The locket lovebirds." Leaning closer, I read, "Eliza Ormiston and Alonzo Pyle. Did they marry?"

Thelma turned the monitor back and clicked some more. I stepped around the desk to make viewing easier. "Here's the bad news," she said.

The missing person listing took up nearly half the newspaper page. Eliza's photo featured prominently, along with other identifying details. She was just 23 years old when she disappeared. "How awful," I said.

"It was a presumed elopement. Their match was forbidden by both families. I was young and my parents tried to keep it quiet. They didn't want to glamorize romance of any kind." Thelma smoothed her velour sleeves and sighed. "They succeeded so well in building my skepticism that I trusted no one."

The hint of bitterness in her voice made Keats rest his muzzle on her pant leg. She scratched his ears absentmindedly, seeming to draw comfort nonetheless.

"Why was their relationship forbidden?" I asked.

"Family feud, as was often the case then. Their fathers crossed swords, probably over a crime."

"Do you know what became of the couple?"

Thelma shook her head. "And not for lack of trying. Like most girls, I had a romantic streak. Unlike most young girls, I knew how to do my research. Later, of course, I had a network of librarians to help me fill in many gaps. Never this one, I'm afraid. Until now, perhaps."

"The bones under the pumpkins." I pressed my hand to my heart. "How tragic. I assume her father did it."

Thelma clicked a few more times, bringing up images of civic leaders in front of town hall. "I'm not so sure. Nelson Ormiston served as mayor for a term. Never smiled. I saw him as a bereft father."

"Well, what about Alonzo's father, then?"

"Possible, I suppose. Hard to imagine a man would kill his only son over a woman, but those feuds ran deep."

I paced back and forth, hand still over my heart. "What about a Romeo and Juliet scenario? Maybe the young couple ended their lives and the parents covered it up."

"Also possible, but it would have been the only such case in Thistledown history. We're an unromantic lot. There were tragedies galore but not the type people write plays about."

She clicked a few times and jabbed her finger at the screen. "That's Alonzo Pyle, Senior. He ran the general store and post office. My father said more got trafficked through that store than dry goods. But Mr. Pyle had a smile for everyone, so I always figured his son got away. Had perhaps even murdered Eliza." Dropping her hand to Keats again, she added, "Perhaps I misjudged the young man because of his mustache. It was the fashion of the day, but I find them terribly unsanitary."

"Where are their families now?" I asked.

She turned the monitor away from me. "That's something for the police to sort out, Ivy. It was dangerous to cross that line back then and might still be today. I suggest we let sleeping dogs lie and focus on the rescue dogs we're helping to place this weekend."

"But I think that locket fell into my hands for a reason, Thelma."

There was a chattering song in my sleeve and Thelma's eyes bulged behind her glasses. "What was that, Ivy?"

"Millicent, my new friend. I believe she was stating her objection to letting sleeping dogs lie. Although it's hard to imagine she'd want to get close to dogs who are awake and alert."

Thelma pushed her chair back and I was glad she did. Otherwise, her scream may well have deafened me when Millicent shot out of my sleeve and raced across the desk. The mouse scrambled over the keyboard and images flicked wildly on the screen, landing once more on Eliza's face. She was attractive, though as unsmiling as her father. Perhaps she was already lovelorn when she posed for the portrait.

"Ivy Rose Galloway. There is a mouse on my keyboard. Just sitting there, full of cheek, and your pets haven't moved a muscle. Did you knowingly bring vermin into my library?"

I shifted Percy from one arm to the other. It wasn't true he hadn't moved. I felt a tremor pass through him as he resisted his instincts to deal with the mouse. "I suppose so, Thelma. She hitched a ride after delivering the locket to me."

"Delivering it? I hardly think that's possible. She's the size of my palm."

As Thelma was pushing her chair further away, she couldn't make a fair comparison.

"True, nevertheless," I said. "The chain was caught around her hind paw and she's been dragging it around. That's what Olive Redding heard in the house. And the owners before her."

"How... curious. And now you're laboring under the impression she wants your help?"

I shrugged. "It wouldn't be the first time an animal came to me to bring justice after a crime. Although obviously Millicent wasn't alive when Eliza passed. Perhaps there have been generations of mice guarding that locket."

Thelma was as far away as she could get without leaving her own office. "I see you've bought into the Disney version of Cinderella, with fanciful cartoon mice dancing about and helping to save the day. People don't make movies about Thistledown rodents, either."

"Millicent is as worthy as any other animal of being heard," I said. "I highly doubt she'd hitch a ride with me if she didn't have something important to communicate. It would be risky even without my pets."

"Ivy, I've gone along with some farfetched stories, but like many, I draw the line at mice. I don't believe a creature of that size could have a brain with much computing power."

Maybe not, but Millicent was working the computer itself rather nicely. She raced back to me, striking the keys as she moved and causing a dizzying array of images. By the time the furry creature shot back up my sleeve, the screen had filled with the image of a woman a few years younger than Thelma, who had a bright smile and gray hair with vivid blue and green highlights.

"Who's that?" I asked, reluctant to bend for a closer look until I figured out where the mouse would settle.

Thelma didn't need to lean in. "That's Vikki Tickle. A local party planner."

I was disappointed. "So, no link to Eliza Ormiston?"

"Tickle is her married name. Victoria is Eliza's younger sister. And they grew up in the house that now belongs to Olive."

Lifting my arm, I stared into the depths of my sleeve. "Millicent, I think Thelma wants to apologize for calling you stupid."

The librarian glared at me. "I will not apologize to a mouse, especially in my own domain." She clicked a few times, printed off a page and handed it to me. "But I never called her stupid. That would be crass." Getting to her feet, she smoothed her velour. "And rather rich coming from someone who enjoys reality shows."

"Thank you, Thelma." I let Keats herd me out of her office. "Go back to your fainting couch."

She followed me through the library and stopped at the outer door. "Please assure me you have that rodent secure."

I tuned into the tiny claws on my shoulder and nodded. "Percy's been temporarily demoted."

The cat let out a soulful wail, which produced a chittering response inside my coat.

Thelma assisted me out rather abruptly and closed the door with something close to a slam. In case I missed the point, she tapped the "Closed" sign.

Her librarian pucker was absolute perfection.

CHAPTER FOURTEEN

Olive Redding looked uncomfortable sitting between Edna and Gertie in the back seat of the truck as we drove along Main Street the next morning. Cori Hogan had tasked Jilly and me with spending time with the Redding sisters separately and deciding if either was worthy of owning a Mafia dog. The hubbub around the haunted house was working against Olive. The dogs that came into the rescue's care were battle weary and needed a calm owner and a stable environment.

"I'm not going to win a dog," Olive said, as if reading my mind. "Cori doesn't like me."

"Cori doesn't like anyone except Bridget," Jilly said, from the passenger seat. "She tolerates the rest of us, depending on need."

"Well, she said I come with 'too much baggage.' She doesn't place her dogs with divorced people."

Jilly's curls swished. "That's not true. The Mafia places dogs with single people if they have the time and commitment to train. They're more suspicious of new couples. If a romance sours, the dog is often returned and it's a heartbreak all around."

Olive's reflection in the rearview mirror brightened. "I have all the time in the world to devote to a dog. But I don't trust myself to choose the right one after choosing the wrong man. That's why I entered this competition."

"Even if the timing doesn't work out, you'll connect with the right dog if you're patient," I said. "Keats fell into my lap on exactly the right day. My best friend here told me to stop walking, and when I did, there he was."

Keats gave a happy rumble from Jilly's lap and turned to give her a poke in the cheek. "You're very welcome, my friend,' she said. "Little did we know then what adventures awaited us."

After a few minutes, Olive spoke again. "So, you're convinced my house isn't haunted, Ivy?"

"Pretty much. It was a rodent, after all. But not just any rodent. There's something very special about Millicent."

She shivered and crossed her arms. "I'm not big on mice."

"You and me both," Jilly said, clutching Percy and Keats a little tighter. "Let's not even get started on the bats."

"I had no idea there were bats in the attic and I looked in that closet dozens of times. The trapdoor you mentioned wasn't open then." Olive clutched herself tighter. "Do you think someone else broke in?"

Keats' paw twitched, suggesting that's exactly what happened, but Gertie spoke up. "The police probably left it open when they took a look around," she said. "That young keener would have been curious."

"Maybe. But I can't live there anymore. Too much weirdness."

"Don't be so hasty," Edna said. "It's a nice big house for the money, and you could put all this behind you in time. Bats and mice are easily eradicated." Before I could protest, she added, "Humanely relocated, I mean. The bat population has been hard hit in recent years. It's a miracle there were half a dozen to fly at Chief Hottie." She gave a chuckle. "How I wish I'd seen that."

"Me too," Gertie said.

"Not me." Jilly sounded horrified. "If I never see a bat up close, that'll suit me fine."

Edna chuckled again. "They're like mice with leathery wings. You'll need to toughen up before the apocalypse, Jillian. Probably earlier, the way Ivy's going. If she's crime-solving with mice, it won't be long till a bat takes the stage."

"Is that what we're doing today?" Olive asked. "Crime-solving? Figuring out whose bones were in the garden?"

"We're just visiting a local party planner," I said. "Thought she might give us some advice on tonight's costume party auction."

"I'm relieved Cori's haunted house fell through," Olive said. "Not sure I could handle fake zombies jumping out at me."

"What about real ones?" Edna asked.

Before Olive could answer, I intervened. "Sounds like the corn husk maze will be scary enough for all of us. Cori told me to wear an adult diaper. Something to keep in mind when choosing a costume later."

I pulled into a pretty cul-de-sac with only a few houses. Vikki Tickle's home was easy to find. It was painted a beautiful blue and had a lot of windows. While there was room at the curb, I turned down the lane beside it. Behind the house was a cottage in a different shade of blue. And behind that was an old food truck that had been custom painted with colorful balloons.

Even the balloons couldn't stop Jilly from groaning. "I hate food trucks."

Many months had passed since people suffered food poisoning after a meal we'd served from just such a truck, but the memory would take far longer to fade.

"That was a trying day," Edna said. "And there are some people I'd like to run over with my ATV. Accidentally on purpose."

I caught her eye in the rearview mirror. "Edna, we have someone new in our midst. Let's not scare Olive with our oddities."

"You have a mouse in your coat," she said. "Which one of us is odder?"

Millicent had spent the night in a ventilated shoebox beside me to keep her safe. She showed no signs of wanting to wander and had popped back into my sleeve at the first opportunity. "Tough one. Jilly's looking pretty good right now."

"Not that good. I'm covered in dog and cat hair." Jilly gave a futile scrape at the fabric of her coat. "I hope Vikki Tickle likes pets."

The smile on Mrs. Tickle's face as she opened her front door said it all. "Oh, how lovely. A dog and a cat!"

"And a mouse," Edna added.

I glared at my friend. Mentioning Millicent was unnecessary as she would likely stay out of sight. People were more repelled by mice than I'd expected. It would be a shame getting off to a poor start when this woman might have valuable information for us.

Vikki's hazel eyes moved from Edna's camouflage to Gertie's poncho, pausing briefly on the rifle. Their outfits seemed to chase the word "mouse" out of her mind and she made way for us to enter the front hall. Vikki's own style choices fell on the eccentric end of the continuum. Her short gray hair had blue and green highlights, and she was wearing a pink blouse with a turquoise cardigan over purple harem pants. Yellow suede slippers completed the ensemble and would be just enough to kick my mother into heart failure. Perhaps they weren't so different though, in liking to stand out in a crowd.

"Mrs. Tickle, we're here on behalf of the rescue dog event," Jilly said. She offered a charming smile and introduced the rest of us. "We heard you're an expert party planner."

"Call me Vikki," she said. "And while I used to be the most popular event planner in the region, I've retired now. My van is up on blocks."

"It's gorgeous," Olive said, finding a smile. "I love the balloons."

"Painted it myself," Vikki said. "I started out doing children's parties, you see, but eventually took on whatever came my way.

Sometimes I lived out of that van for a week at a time." The older woman's smile faded. "I heard animals fighting out back last night. I hope raccoons haven't gotten inside. Be a doll and check on it, would you?"

Olive seemed to be the doll in question and she slipped out the door looking relieved to escape the crowd.

"Come in for tea and tell me how I can help," Vikki said, leading us to the kitchen. "I know all of you by reputation. I've read the news stories." She turned and smiled at Keats. "This dog is a handsome hero."

Keats mumbled a humblebrag and we all laughed. "He agrees wholeheartedly," I said, looking past her to the sliding doors at the rear of the house. "Do you think Olive will be all right out there?"

"Oh, she'll be fine," Vikki said. "A distraction will do her good, poor girl."

Olive circled the truck before nimbly scaling a ladder on the side. I pulled out my phone to snap pictures, knowing her gumption would win points with Cori, especially if animals were involved.

Jilly made small talk about Thistledown and the rescue event as our host put the kettle on and gathered mugs. She opened a package of cookies and dumped them onto a plate, breaking about half of them. Gertie carried the tray of mugs to the table and when the tea was steeping, Vikki followed with the pot in a colorful cozy. Everything in this house was vibrant and cheery. I had the sense that Vikki worked hard to keep up that front. Just the same, her smile faltered and went out when she sat down. "I do love a party, as you can imagine, but I've never been a fan of Halloween. It's a license to misbehave, if you ask me."

Four voices overlapped as we chimed agreement.

"This event is for a good cause, though," Jilly said. "It will fill the rescue coffers for months to come. I hear every room in town is taken."

"I'm sure some of the crowd is here for the dogs," Vikki said, eyeing Percy in Jilly's lap. "But some are here to learn more about what this cat found in the garden of my childhood home."

"No point beating around the bush with a woman like Vikki," Edna said.

"None at all." Vikki's smile flickered back on. "I expected you today. The police are visiting in about an hour, so you have a little time to get your exclusive." Pulling the cozy off the teapot, she filled the mugs. "Of course, I'll need to repeat everything to the police. It's the right thing to do."

"Absolutely," Jilly said. "My husband is leading the investigation."

Nodding, Vikki turned to me. "What about your fiancé? I heard he was in town, too."

"Just to keep tabs on Ivy," Gertie said, with a wink.

Vikki's smile came back in full force. "So that she doesn't beat the police to the best interviews?"

"Basically." I returned her smile. "I get the feeling we're kindred spirits, Vikki."

"I came to the same conclusion when I saw a mouse peeking out of your collar," she said. "People get all worked up about rodents but there are bigger things to worry about in this world."

Edna took a sip of black tea. "I like the cut of your jib, Vikki. I'll make room in my bunker for you when the end comes, although I'm not a fan of harem pants."

"I'm not a fan of camo," Vikki said. "We don't need to agree on everything, do we?"

"No, although it helps," Edna said. "Can you handle an ATV?"

"Yes, indeed. Plus motorcycles and snowmobiles. Even a jet ski, on occasion. When someone wanted a party, I did my very best to deliver."

Picking up a tiny pair of tongs, Vikki dropped a sugar cube in Edna's tea, following it with a bit of milk. Somehow, she knew Edna was deliberately depriving herself of the niceties.

Edna stirred her tea, took a long sip and offered a rare, genuine smile. "It's a shame you retired, Vikki. You can't be more than seventy."

"Seventy-four next month. If it weren't for the cataract, I'd work right to the grave." She topped up Edna's tea. "Some ham-fisted surgeon in Brenton botched the job and I'm basically down one eye."

"They took your license?" Jilly asked.

Vikki shook her head. "I can still drive. Legally." Using the tongs, she added another sugar cube to Edna's mug. "Losing confidence is the kiss of death."

Edna added more milk to dilute the sweet brew. "It doesn't need to be that way. Remember the old expression. When a door closes, a window opens. Sometimes that window belongs to a food truck."

"I just don't feel right about it, anymore. Although I don't like sitting around here, either. Hobbies always seemed like a waste of time."

Edna took the little tongs and added a sugar cube to Vikki's mug. "You just need to find the right hobbies. Useful hobbies. When you know you're doing something for the good of humanity, it helps." Sipping her overly sweet tea, Edna grimaced. "For the good of *good* humanity, that is. You've been on the planet long enough to know the difference."

"I learned that young. In the very house you're all here about." Vikki watched me over the rim of her mug. "You might as well get to the point before the police break up our tea party."

"You're right," I said. "Let me fill you in."

She listened intently to the story, right up to the part where the bats flew at Kellan's head. Then she laughed out loud. "We had bats in the attic at one point. I like to think the ones you met are their descendants. Perhaps even your mouse. I was an animal lover, like you, Ivy. More a dog lover, I suppose, but after my husband died, I couldn't get another because I was on the road too much."

I flipped through my gallery and then pushed the phone across the table. "This is the locket the mouse was dragging around. There were photos inside, plus engraving."

After studying them for a few moments, she pushed the phone back. "That's my sister, yes. I was the last of ten children and around seven when Eliza left."

"Do you know how she died?" I asked, gently.

"Natural causes, I presume." Vikki's eyes had a defiant expression. "I suppose you think my sister has been pushing up pumpkins at the home that young lady now owns." Her thumb jerked toward Olive, who was crawling on top of the truck. "But the bones you found didn't belong to Eliza."

"No? Well, I'm glad to hear that. Do you know who it is?" I considered mentioning the skeleton had company, but since the police were coming, she'd hear it officially soon enough. No need to steal all my brother's thunder.

She shook her head. "I had no idea there was a body out there and I'm glad I didn't. Like most men of that day, my father had enemies, but I never saw him threaten or commit violence."

"I heard a rumor that he wasn't happy about Eliza falling for Alonzo Pyle."

"Rumor is usually wrong but not in this case. My father detested the Pyle family and resisted their marriage, just as he did mine."

"Yours!" The surprises kept coming.

She frowned as she topped up mugs. "He'd mellowed by the time my turn came around, but still forbade me to see Lisle. So I eloped, too, and we settled in Dorset Hills. Eventually, Father thanked me for saving him the cost of a wedding. Said he'd gotten lucky twice."

Jilly leaned forward. "So he thought Eliza eloped, too?"

Vikki nodded. "We all did. It was a shame she never came home because he would have forgiven her, as he did me. She didn't even send my folks postcards."

I looked down at Keats, who'd raised a paw in the direction of the dining room. "Did Eliza send *you* postcards?"

Nodding, she pushed herself up with both hands and walked to a rolltop desk in the adjoining room and pulled out a lower drawer. "They started after I married. Didn't come often, but it was always comforting when they did. My great hope was to meet Eliza again as an adult."

She came back with a stack of postcards bound with a fraying purple velvet ribbon.

"Is it too late?" I asked, letting her place the stack in my open palms. "To see your sister again?"

Her eyes filled with tears and she nodded. "I assume so. About ten years ago, the postcards slowed and finally stopped. Eliza would be around ninety now, if she'd lived."

"That's not old," Edna said. "I intend to pass the century mark. Someone needs to look out for these crazy kids." Using the sugar tongs, she made a snapping motion at the window. "Including that one."

Olive was about to climb down the side of the truck and there was something squirming in her jacket.

"Trouble of the right kind," I said, flipping through the postcards. "These were mailed from all over the country. Didn't they ever settle down?"

Vikki walked to the sliding doors. "I guess not, but the correspondence was a one-way street." Glancing over her shoulder, she saw my fingers flexing over my phone. "Take photos if you like. The police might carry off the postcards."

I didn't give her a chance to change her mind. "I wonder why she didn't at least write to your mother."

"Perhaps Eliza never forgave her for not backing the marriage. Or there may have been more to the story than I knew. My parents mellowed in time, and Lisle and I moved home to Thistledown when Mother needed more help. They'd long since moved from the old house by then." Unlatching the door, she slid open the glass. "We were happy here. My father said Lisle never amounted to much but he was perfect for me. Husbands of his era didn't want their wives gallivanting but Lisle sent me off with a smile. 'Happy wife, happy life,' he always said, and that's what we had."

"May I ask about that little cottage?" Jilly said. "It's so quaint."

Vikki turned back. "Built it for our daughter and she lived there for years. I was determined to be the supportive parent I never had. Guess it worked, because she didn't go far."

Jilly and I left the silent question hanging, but Edna wasn't one for subtlety. "And where is your daughter now?"

"Scattered in the hills, I'm afraid." There was a hitch in Vikki's voice as she turned away. "I wanted her in the family plot but she preferred to blow free with the dogs who went before. I respected her wishes."

"You sound like a wonderful mother." Jilly's voice cracked. "I'm so sorry for your loss."

The old woman ran her fingers through blue and green hair. "Thank you, dear. It was terribly hard, coming just two years after Lisle's passing, but I kept working. Bringing the party to those who needed it until I couldn't."

"There's a party coming your way now," Edna said. "Or a predator. Hard to say."

It was a little of both. When Olive stepped through the open door, there were bloody gashes on her cheek, neck and hands. "Ungrateful little goblin didn't want to be saved," she said, unzipping her jacket a little. A fluffy black head popped up and eerie yellow eyes glared at all of us, but especially Percy. The two cats hissed at each other, one tiny, the other puffed nearly as big as a pumpkin. "He's feral. What are we going to do with him?"

"Feral?" Edna said. "That's nothing compared to what I saw in my colony. If you managed to snag this fellow and stick him in your coat, you have a friend for life."

"I already have a cat," Olive said. "I'm trying to win a dog in this competition, remember?"

"Cori and the others can find this little guy a home," Jilly said. "He's so cute."

The kitten was far from cute. Goblin was a very apt name but Jilly had a soft spot for felines.

"I've heard them say it's difficult to place black cats, especially around Halloween," I said. "How about you, Vikki?"

She shook her head. "You don't take on kittens at my age. This one will outlive me. I do miss having a pet for companionship, though."

Olive kept running her hand over her coat, murmuring sweet nothings to the feisty feline. "How about we go halves on him? He'll live with you but I'll take care of the vet visits and see to his needs. If I move out of town, we'll reconsider."

Vikki tipped her head. "You're selling my childhood home? Is it because of the bats or the bones?"

"Both," Olive said. "I don't think I'll be able to forget them. My realtor will need to foist it on some poor sucker, but of course I'll fully disclose its history."

"Someone will be glad to get it," Edna said. "Although you'll take a loss, I'm afraid."

Olive shrugged. "Lost a husband, lost a house, gained half a cat."

"And maybe a full dog," I said.

Vikki laughed. "I like your attitude, Olive. We'll share Goblin for now."

Jilly picked up Percy and squeezed his fluff down. "Be careful, Vikki. Cat scratches can be slow to heal."

"Oh, he won't scratch me," she said, stretching out her hands. "Goblin, enough. You climbed on my truck for a reason so have some manners."

Doubt crossed Olive's face as she unzipped further and pulled out the scrawniest kitten I'd ever seen. He continued to hiss as she passed him to the old woman. When he landed in Vikki's hands, he calmed considerably. The hissing stopped but his high-pitched growl rolled on, directed alternately at Percy and then Keats. The latter gave a pant-laugh, that basically said, "Good luck with that."

"He has brought me luck," Vikki said, almost as if she understood my dog. "I had a rough night after hearing about the bones but look how things turned around today. New friends and half a cat." The kitten turned in her arms and opened his mouth in a silent hiss. "Goblin, you're a prince."

Jilly and I grinned at each other. Vikki was our people.

Keats' ears flicked and he mumbled a warning. Millicent gave a little cheep, too. The atmosphere was shifting.

Tucking the kitten into her cardigan, Vikki started collecting mugs with her free hand. "I imagine that's your cue, ladies. The police are likely on their way."

I checked her clock and nodded. "You really don't have an idea of who ended up under the pumpkins, Vikki?"

She shook her head. "I'll put some thought into it. In the meantime, I suggest you drive straight out past the cottage. There's a private lane."

"Awesome," I said, heading for the back door.

"You don't have to lie to my husband," Jilly said. "In fact, I'd prefer you didn't."

The mugs clinked as Vikki put them in the dishwasher. "I don't make a practice of lying to the police. But I enjoy keeping them on their toes. It's good for them. And husbands, too."

Everyone laughed except Olive. "That must be where I went wrong. My sister says I'm a pleaser."

"So easily fixed," Vikki said. "Look at Goblin. He's absolutely obnoxious and we're falling all over him. You can learn from this cat."

Olive laughed, and it was probably the first time she'd really let her guard down since we'd met. "If you say so."

"I do. And we'll have plenty of time to chat when you're over here scooping litter. That's something I don't dare do at this point. I'm afraid you'd find me face down and lifeless. There are better ways to go."

"And worse," Edna said. "Helping an animal is a noble cause. Even a mouse."

"Especially a mouse," I said, although I didn't feel at all noble with little paws skittering around in my coat. Millicent had become agitated when Goblin joined us. "This one may hold the secret to the deaths at your family home, Vikki."

"Please take a good look around the house before selling it," she said. "That locket was one of many lovely gifts from Alonzo, as I recall. If Eliza left without the necklace, the other pieces could be hidden there, too."

"I will," Olive said. "Promise."

Vikki walked to the back door. She cradled the kitten in her sweater and Goblin's eyes came up over her collar. I thought he looked a little smug.

Edna slipped a card under the teapot on the counter before going. "You have many good years ahead, Vikki."

The smile on the older woman's face faltered again. "I hope so, but I'll wager the person under the pumpkins thought so, too."

CHAPTER FIFTEEN

The Thistledown Festival was everything a fall fair should be, with an overlay of Halloween that nearly tipped the balance into tawdry. Jilly clucked in disgust over the decorations but it wasn't long before she was cooing instead. The witch hats, skeletons and ghosts lost all power once she noticed the displays of artisanal products, ranging from cheese to preserves to soap. Jilly had tried several times to get a line of Runaway Inn products off the ground, but something always intervened. Specifically, murder. Creation generally took a back seat to cremation, it seemed. When we weren't solving a murder we were worrying about the next one. The adrenaline rarely let up.

Keats mumbled something that sounded mocking. This dog was fully present in his life, doing exactly what he wanted to do. That was his personal philosophy and he urged me to adopt it.

"Yeah, whatever," I said. "Let's just enjoy the fair. I want a caramel apple."

"Is he talking to you?" Kestra Redding asked, following so closely she ran into me when I stopped at a stand. "The dog, I mean?"

"Sort of. Not really. He mumbles and I interpret as suits the occasion." I turned to Jilly. "They only have candy apples."

"Hold out for caramel," she said. "I doubt I'll have time to make you any this year."

"I thought you hated Halloween," Edna said, rolling her eyes at me.

"I do. And I love caramel apples. They're not mutually exclusive."

She scowled at me. "They most certainly are. Candy, caramel and chocolate do not belong on apples. An apple is perfect unto itself." She pulled one out of her pocket and took a bite. "I got this Macintosh from your own orchard, whereas you've been buying fancy hybrids from the gourmet store."

"I like my apples a little sweeter. Hence the caramel coating. But when the apocalypse comes, you can be sure I'll appreciate those Macs."

"I appreciate them now," Jilly said. "I managed to put up some apple chutney last week. Feels like I just get into a groove when murder intervenes."

"Exactly what I was telling Keats." I turned to Kestra. "But not really."

"Olive mentioned you guys were interesting," she said. "And Halloween haters. Meanwhile I love everything about it." She did a girlish twirl. "The jack-o'-lanterns, the costumes, the masks... all of it. But I'm a sucker for any holiday."

I looked around at my friends. "She's from Oppositeville."

"That's because I grew up at Howler Hall. No holiday is too small to be celebrated. We do it up big there with crafts, cookery, choir and so much more."

Edna looked at Gertie and smirked. "More room in the bunker for us."

"I don't have to understand that to know it's an insult," Kestra said. "But we're all a product of our upbringing, no? I've embraced my holiday trauma instead of resisting it." She smirked, too. "You two wear camo and ponchos and I wear themed sweaters." Unzipping her coat, she revealed a different hand-knitted sweater—this time a black cardigan featuring orange witches on broomsticks. "It's how you wear it, am I right? Are we really so different?"

Gertie and Edna stared at each other, digesting this. "Yes," Gertie said. "You're annoyingly perky. That's about as different from us as can be."

Kestra laughed. "It's a coping mechanism. Like naming a rifle. And bragging about riding big machines. But I've had enough therapy to know that."

"Ivy," Edna said. "You have duct tape in your go-kit. We're going to need it."

"You can silence me," Kestra said, "but you can't unhear what I said." She pointed from Edna to Gertie and back. "Tonight, you'll lie awake wondering... 'Is my fearsome getup just a more insidious version of a holiday sweater?'"

Jilly and I glanced at each other, torn between amusement and horror. It was unusual for anyone to goad Gertie and Edna outright, especially on early acquaintance. Did Kestra Redding have a death wish? Or was she truly just as quirky as them but in deceptively normal garb? Normal in some circles, that is. Not mine.

"You're not going to win one of the Mafia's dogs," Edna said. "I don't say that to be mean, although mean never stops me. I just want you to moderate your expectations. You're too—"

"Eccentric?" Kestra interrupted. "No worse than you."

"Maybe not, but the Mafia hasn't placed a dog with me, and wouldn't. Gertie, either. If you truly wanted to win this competition, you'd be hiding your freak light under a bushel."

Kestra zipped her coat again. "I probably should but I've made my peace with losing. My real goal in coming was to support my sister and reconnect." Her smile faded a little. "Olive's not a fan of my freak light, either."

"You're quite different," I said. "Were you really raised apart?"

"Pretty much, yeah. And she thinks I got the better deal having the run of Howler Hall and Gran's full attention. But getting turfed out of my family didn't feel good. We became more like cousins."

"Families are never easy," I said, and all my friends muttered agreement. "It's better not to depend on them too much. Choose the people who choose you. I built an awesome friend-family when I moved home to Clover Grove. A dog is a great place to start but unless you get as lucky as I did with Keats, you need more."

"Where is home for you now, Kestra?" Jilly asked.

"Boston. Or at least it was, until I lost my job this morning. Replaced by A.I." Jilly and I exchanged an uneasy look. We were hearing this story more and more and it was disheartening. A.I. wasn't even on the radar when we worked in the human resources field. "Before that I had other contracts that ended for the same reason."

"That's ridiculous," Edna said. "Artificial intelligence will be no help at all to people when the apocalypse comes. Meanwhile the human brain will atrophy at an increasing rate until we're little better than zombies ourselves."

"I agree with you, Miss Evans. And right now, I have no idea what to try next." Kess stared around at the various stands in the market row. "Maybe starting my own business would be the way to go, but I'm one of those jack-of-all-trades types. Master of none." Her heavy sigh fluttered some tall peacock feathers standing in a jar on an otherwise vacant vendor table. "And yes, I know that makes me a poor choice in the rescue competition—especially if I lose my apartment. But I won't lie about my situation."

Jilly patted her shoulder. "Honesty is definitely the best policy. Besides, Keats and Percy are lie detectors."

I expected the dog to brag a little about his skills, but his ears were flattening and his ruff rising. Percy struggled to get down from Jilly's arms, looking decidedly disgruntled as well. There was a sign on the vacant vendor table that said, "Back in Five Minutes." Other than the feathers, the wares appeared to be packed in cartons underneath.

"Your pets think something stinks at the fall fair," Edna said. "Worse than the candy apples."

A woman wearing an apron emerged from the growing crowd, stepped around the table, and said, "You. Move along now. My products are not for sale."

"Hello again, Ms. Mushing," I said. "What's the purpose of renting a table at a fair and not selling your products?"

"I'll sell what I brought." She started pulling boxes out from under the table. "Just not to you or your cronies. Or your handy cop relative."

I tried a mollifying smile. "I know we got off on the wrong foot, but I did buy four items from your store, remember?"

She set up some candles and various scents collided above the table. "Two of which were on hold for another client who was terribly disappointed."

"The Sprockets seemed glad for us to have them," Jilly said. "We caught up with them before they left town."

Blenda didn't look surprised. "Never fear, I'll ship what they need. I always go the extra distance for a good customer."

"It's a shame none of your special charms were able to help the Sprockets," I said. "I know they tried to address some issues at their house before selling to Olive Redding."

The storekeeper flipped her long hair, which had frizzed greatly in the fall dampness. "They gave up too easily. You don't just sage a house once and call it done. There are steps involved in clearing a house properly. I wish the Sprockets better luck with their new house."

"You might still have a chance to salvage the old one," Kestra chimed in. "Paige Ogilvy is trying to reverse the sale because of my sister's distress over the situation."

Blenda's pale eyes grew cagey. "Your sister shouldn't be too hasty. That's a lovely house and I'm sure we could clear any spiritual residue." She plucked a card out of her apron pocket and handed it to Kestra. "Tell your sister I'd be happy to assess the house again. With the skeleton gone from the yard, it should be simple enough to freshen the energy." Reaching into the jar, she plucked out a peacock feather. "Start by opening all the windows and walking through the house while sweeping this around." She handed it to Kestra, along with a scroll tied with black ribbon. "Repeat this verse three times in each room."

"A spell?" Kestra asked. "We don't go in for that stuff."

Blenda tossed her frizzy hair. "Suit yourself. It's worked well for others."

"Like us," someone said. I turned to see a young man and woman who looked familiar. It took me a moment to place them as competitors in the rescue event. "Our house didn't feel like home till we invited Blenda over to do some energy work."

"Is that like feng shui?" I said.

"Nothing like that." Blenda was indignant. "Feng shui is a marketing ploy meant to part gullible people from their money."

"And peacock feathers are science?" Kestra asked. She was a cheeky one, and Cori, unfortunately, would clip her wings and give a dog to this couple. Despite their apparent fondness for Blenda, they seemed like ideal pet owners. They were dressed like the models in an upscale country casual magazine and each held a steaming cup of cider. The man was also carrying a candy apple with a bite out of either side, as if they'd had a joint nibble for a photo op. This was about as small-town wholesome as you could get, at least until their dream dog joined them and a stroller rolled into the picture. The Redding sisters weren't conventional enough to get the rescue stamp of approval.

"None of this is a science," Blenda Mushing said. "But you can't beat word of mouth."

Keats gave me a poke in the shin and I switched on an HR smile.

He moved me away with the picture-perfect couple, while Jilly herded Kestra in the other direction. Meanwhile, Millicent fired off some squeaks from the little carrier I'd created from a hard-sided castoff purse of Maud Gentry's and strapped tightly across my midriff. It would never get me into an upscale country magazine but it might keep my passenger safe.

When we were out of Blenda's earshot, I introduced myself properly to Mika and Matt Hull, and then said, "If you don't mind sharing, I'd love to know what happened at your house to make you hire Blenda."

Mika Hull leaned in and whispered, "The place was haunted. At least, we think so. Doors slammed, objects were moved, and there were sounds in the night. Twice we saw footprints inside the house that didn't belong to us, although there was no sign of a break-in." She squeezed my wrist. "I wanted to sell and move back to Dorset Hills. Can you blame me?"

"Not at all. I'd want to move, too." I pressed the mouse carrier close to my jacket to drown out Millicent's contributions to the conversation.

"We couldn't afford to buy in Dorset Hills, though," Matt Hull said, picking up the story. "And we wanted a big house, with room for children and pets. When our house came on the market at a reasonable price, it seemed too good to be true."

His wife sipped her cider and then coughed. "It *was* too good to be true. I barely got a wink of sleep for weeks. So, we went back to Paige Ogilvy and told her to sell it."

"And Paige discouraged you?"

"Not at first," Mika said. "She got into quite a dustup with Glennis Redding and we didn't know whether we were coming or going for a couple of weeks."

Matt downed his cider with a gulp and dropped the cup in a trash can. "Glennis said we'd regret it. That we'd never find a place like this again."

"It was a risk I was willing to take," Mika said, finishing her drink, too. "There are worse things than renting."

"But you stuck it out," I prompted. "What changed?"

"Paige convinced us to move into a motel for a week," Mika said. "She hired someone out of her own pocket to do some painting inside and landscaping outside. Then she paid for Blenda Mushing to do her thing. By the time we moved back, it felt like a different house." Matt offered her the candy apple and she took a bite before mumbling, "I feel safe there now."

Matt rubbed her shoulder. "I didn't want to buy into the woo-woo stuff but it really does feel different and we agreed to keep the house. Especially since housing prices in Thistledown are climbing like crazy."

Grabbing my arm, Mika nudged the mouse carrier and a squeak made her step back. "Blenda is worth a try before Olive gives up. You have to experience it to believe it."

"Huh," I said. "So this peacock feather thing is for real?"

Matt took the candy apple back from his wife with a sheepish smile. "Guess so."

Keats wasn't buying it. He gave his blue eye a workout on both Mika and Matt and got nowhere, however. They weren't lying. It just might not be the actual truth.

Wiping sticky fingers with a napkin, the woman said, "Why not come over this afternoon and see for yourself?"

Keats accepted the invitation with a mumble and my thanks were merely a formality. The dog moved them closer to the trash can and Matt dropped the apple into the bin.

"They always taste better in your head," Mika said. "But I fall for it every year."

I laughed. "Same."

Matt used his sleeve to wipe his forehead. "The combination of sweet and sour made my brain buzz."

I took their contact information and watched them walk away, hand in hand. Keats mumbled something disparaging, that made me wonder if they were as perfect as they seemed. Maybe he'd expose a flaw in their glossy veneer this afternoon and put the Reddings back in the race.

Millicent squeaked again and I realized she'd probably been trying to get my attention. I was used to more assertive animals.

Suddenly, a scream ripped out over the cool air.

And it didn't sound human.

CHAPTER SIXTEEN

"Keats, come!" someone called. Not Jilly. Not Edna, nor Gertie.

It was Kestra Redding.

That was the first surprise.

The second surprise was that my dog obeyed. He usually heeded Jilly, Maud and Cori. Kellan, only if it was official business. Edna and Gertie occasionally got good service if he was feeling magnanimous, or happened to want the same thing they did. Strangers? Not a chance. At least, I couldn't recall such instances as I followed him behind the vendor tables where boxes, baskets and folding chairs had tipped over.

"What's going on?" I asked, catching the edge of Gertie's poncho.

"There's a bird on the loose," she said. "A big one. A loud one."

Jilly hurried through an obstacle course to reach me, dragging Kestra Redding behind her, while Percy squirmed under her other arm. "It's a peacock belonging to Blenda Mushing," my best friend said. "Kestra released it."

"Why on earth would you do that, Kestra?" I crouched to watch my dog dart under tables and around people as he began herding the shrieking bird. He got it moving but didn't bring it back toward Blenda's table. The bird ran ahead of him and away from us. I thought about calling him back, but he must have had his reasons and I'd catch up with him shortly.

The bird didn't take flight, despite the trees dotting the vendor area. My peacock knowledge was limited but there'd been enough "lost" signs posted around Clover Grove to tell me they could wing it when they wished.

"I had to let it go," Kestra said. "Blenda has been stripping its tail feathers. Causing him harm."

Blenda Mushing was now chasing my dog, who was chasing the bird. This wouldn't end well for someone, quite possibly me. "What makes you say that?"

Kestra was too distracted by the circus to answer, so Jilly did. "We overheard Blenda talking on the phone to someone who was coming to get the bird. She said its tail feathers didn't grow anymore, so it was of no use to her. She needs them for her so-called energy work."

"I had a bad feeling about the buyer and the bird," Kestra said. "A few years ago I worked in marketing for the fashion sector. A designer who used peacock feathers in his work ended up in the news because they weren't naturally shed. Advocates exposed him for inhumane practices."

I prodded Kestra ahead of me in the peacock parade. "You think Blenda is doing the same?"

"There's no reason for a peacock to stop growing its train naturally," she said. "Every year those feathers molt and come back longer and fuller. But if people are impatient or the bird is injured—"

I was relieved when someone accidentally shoved Kestra and interrupted the story. I didn't want to hear the details.

Regaining her balance, Kestra said, "Anyway, I won't stand by and allow people to treat birds inhumanely. Or anything else, for that matter. So I set him free."

Her face was flushed and I had no doubt she thought she'd made the right move.

"But you don't know for a fact that's happening, Kestra," Jilly said. "You're not the bird police."

"Even if you're right," I picked up, "there are more subtle and effective ways to handle these things. Blenda didn't need to see this coming."

Jilly gave me a warning look. "Don't encourage her, Ivy."

"It's a job for experts," I continued. "And I don't know about you, but I'm no expert on peacocks. Now there's one on the loose in late fall. What if we can't get him back? The nights are cold."

Her lips pressed together but she was still defiant. "Keats will get him back. Cori said he was a master herder. Almost as good as her dog."

A defiant bark drifted back, as if Keats protested being bested even by Cori's prizewinning sheepdog.

"Keats has great chops," I said. "But one creature that has evaded him is a very large bird. A flightless bird. And that's on the farm. Here, Keats is in unfamiliar territory."

"But this peacock can't fly," Kestra persisted. "Blenda said she'd clipped his wing, too."

Edna shouted up ahead, "Got him!"

I assumed she meant the bird and started to head over. Jilly's sleeve came down across my path like the barrier at a railway crossing. "You two... leave this to me."

She strode to Blenda. The vendor's arms were flapping angrily and the irony struck me. If Kestra was right, Blenda's wings had just been clipped, too. Harming animals garnered negative press in most hill country communities now.

I gestured for Kestra to stay quiet so that I could hear Blenda's explanation. She insisted the peacock's feathers were damaged in a barnyard brawl. The bird was getting bullied by other peafowl and she was finding him a happier, safer home.

It was a plausible story. But Keats, who was positioned between the two women, shot me a look to say it wasn't the truth, or at least the full truth. As further proof, Blenda did not suggest calling police to back her up. She would likely settle quietly. Loudly, but quietly.

Kestra tried to go over and I shook my head. "Leave it to Jilly. In the meantime, tell me your plan for this bird. Are you taking it to your apartment in Boston?"

She deflated considerably and then scuffed the earth with her sneaker. "I'll probably need to give up my apartment after losing my job. Guess I'll be couch surfing with a big bird."

I wanted to laugh but managed to choke it back. "Birds take a special touch, Kestra. A lot of knowledge. Their care is daunting to me, and I have quite a variety of animals."

"If Blenda Mushing can keep a peacock alive, I can." Her eyes met mine and dropped again. "I guess that's the point. She wasn't caring for it well. I would need to do far better."

Giving her a cool stare, I asked, "Were you assuming I'd take the purloined peacock? You wouldn't be the first to consider Runaway Farm a dumping ground."

"I didn't assume *anything*. I just wanted to help the bird."

I continued to stare at her and I didn't need my discerning sheepdog to tell me she was being honest. Kestra was impetuous and soft-hearted when it came to animals... like me. Maybe she'd been conked on the head at some point, too. Otherwise, she should have more impulse control. But I wasn't in a position to find fault. If I'd known the bird was being harmed—and for such a silly scheme—I would very likely have helped, too. But now I had friends who would moderate my rash impulses. More than half the time, I could be persuaded not to do something quite so brash.

"Now it's on us to fix this," I said. "If you're jobless and couch surfing, I assume you don't have money to buy off Blenda."

She scuffed the earth harder. "I'll sell my car. Olive can front me the cash."

"Your sister isn't flush, either. She's jobless and potentially couch surfing too, until this house situation is resolved. It's not her problem." I gestured to Jilly. "It's become ours."

Kestra's face flushed again, this time from embarrassment. "I'm sorry. Can you cover it till I sell my car? I'll find a good home for the peacock. Cori will probably know the right place."

I towed her further from the fray. "Cori will probably rehome it with me, as usual. Another big flightless bird is just what I need."

Jilly was holding her ground with both Blenda and what I assumed was the bird-buyer. Gertie was making sure everyone played nice by brandishing Minnie around, while Edna stood back holding what I assumed was a bird under a white tablecloth festooned with black cats, bats and witch's hats.

"I'm going over," Kestra said, trying to get around me and failing.

"No, you're letting cooler heads prevail. That's a lesson I'm still learning, and if I could give you one piece of unsolicited advice it would be to surround yourself with the right people. Hotheads like us need a big buffer."

"I'm not a hothead," she muttered. "Usually."

I glanced over my shoulder as I herded her even further away. "That's earned more unsolicited advice. I suggest you start by admitting your failings. *Then* find your buffers. And cross your fingers that one of those buffers is a great dog."

What little spark she had left went out. "I'll never win a dog now. I *am* a hothead."

It was time to ease up a little. "Look, Kess. People end up hotheads for various reasons. No need to tell me yours. But it didn't stop me from finding the very best dog for me—and I didn't need Cori Hogan's help to do it."

"You took on a killer to get him. I read about it."

"There are far easier ways, and I promise I will help if you just keep a lid on it till this peacock situation is resolved."

"I'll look after the peacock. I stand behind my decisions."

I rubbed my forehead. She was enough to make me despair, and for a moment, I got a very good idea of how Jilly and Kellan must feel about me sometimes. I was not only hotheaded but hardheaded.

Keats arrived under my other hand and gave a ha-ha-ha. I let out a long sigh, knowing the matter must be resolved.

The rest of my buffer was heading toward us. Jilly's face was bright pink from swallowing too much pride. Edna's was furrowed in frustration from being hamstrung by an armful of peacock. And Gertie was smirking from the sheer joy of intimidating shifty people with her rifle.

Percy crouched to pounce on me but I shook my head and patted Millicent's carrier. His tail lashed in annoyance and he launched at Kestra instead. She didn't flinch as he landed. On the contrary, she reached up and scratched the cat's ears as he head-butted her with a fair bit of force.

"An apology would be a good first step in owning your issues," I said.

"Sorry, Percy and Keats," she said, earning herself a mumbled reprimand. "Thank you for stepping in to handle the mess I made. And I'm sorry to the rest of you, as well. Ivy's given me quite a lecture on setting my life right. After taking responsibility, I've got to find some good friends. A buffer."

"Good friends with deep pockets," Jilly said. "You owe me four hundred bucks for that peacock, Kestra. Plus room and board at the farm till you have a place for it."

Edna stomped ahead of us as we went back to the truck. "Friends like us are hard to find, young lady. We're a rare breed."

"Oh, I know." Kestra's voice got stronger as she rallied. "Especially since my friends need to love holidays. All of them. Including Halloween."

Edna turned and thrust the swaddled peacock into Kestra's arms. "Over to you. That thing ejects guano. Good thing you have backup sweaters."

CHAPTER SEVENTEEN

J illy and I decided to visit the young couple from the fair on our way to the costume rental store later that afternoon. We'd hoped to reverse the two visits, but the peacock situation had delayed us. It was a shame the bird got loose again in the truck. In the end, Edna, Gertie and Jilly had walked back to the library with Percy, leaving Kess to hold the bird and me to clean up.

My weekend away from animals was just a weekend with new animals. Oddly enough, I didn't mind. It just made for complicated logistics. Maud kindly offered to house the peacock temporarily and I had to make a couple of trips for supplies, and to get people to the right place. By the time I escaped with Jilly, time was running away on us.

"We're taking a risk," my best friend said, as we pulled out of Maud's driveway. "All the good costumes will be gone, Ivy. I'm not going to that party dressed as a gargoyle."

"Of course not. If there's a gargoyle costume, I'm taking it. You can be a fairytale princess. So many to choose from, right?"

She was slightly mollified but still irked. "I don't see why we need to dress up at all. Our contestants aren't going to win."

"The Reddings may be long shots for this competition, but I like both sisters," I said. "Their hearts are in the right place."

"Their heads are in the wrong place. Olive is still reeling from her divorce and the impulsive decision to buy a fixer-upper. And Kess is just a wild card. No job, no home and no impulse control." She glanced at me. "And don't you dare lump yourself into Kess's category. You were never that bad."

"Jilly, my friend, I have a mouse in my blouse. If that isn't bad, I don't know what is."

"You would never be caught dead in a blouse. Let alone a Halloween sweater."

I turned down a pretty street not far from Vikki Tickle's house. "I borrowed a tight thermal top from Louisa with a kangaroo pocket and put Millicent in there. Just don't kick me in the gut."

She finally cracked a smile. "It's not you I want to kick. But what was wrong with the purse pack? That seemed like a good option for mouse transport."

"Millicent was very vocal at the fair. I think she was uncomfortable. So I left Maud and Lou to figure out something better for tonight. An auction is the perfect time to get the scuttlebutt, especially in disguise. Someone knows more about what happened at Olive's house. I'm sure of it."

"Asher might be making some progress," she said. "He was in a good mood when we spoke earlier."

I glanced at her. "No leaks?"

She shook her head. "My wiles hit a brick wall. At times like this, I really need to cook something and replenish my charm bank."

"Tomorrow, when we get home, you can hit the kitchen hard while I get the sisters sorted out."

"The sisters?" She sounded startled. "Olive and Kess?"

I laughed. "Lucy and Ethel. The goats. They were feuding when I left."

"Sisters," she said. "Hard enough having a close cousin."

We parked and took our time checking out the front of the house before heading up the stairs. It was a larger and nicer house than Olive's, though of similar vintage. Previous owners had maintained it well. Only in seeing this one did I realize how much work Olive would need to do to bring it to a level she'd really enjoy, and she didn't seem like the type to appreciate the process. She was anxious and there was nothing calming about renovations.

Mika and Matt Hull welcomed us warmly into their home and took us on the grand tour through spacious and tastefully furnished rooms.

I lagged behind and consulted the pets in a whisper. "What do you think, boys? It does have a different vibe to Olive's house."

Keats mumbled something inconclusive. The place was not in the clear as far as he was concerned.

Percy, on the other hand, swatted the peacock feather standing in a tall vase near the front door. He did the same to the one in the hall upstairs. I hated to think those had come from an abused bird, especially when the homeowners had been sold peacock poppycock. A feather alone would not banish evil. I'd seen too much of it to believe it could be that simple.

Millicent was so still inside her pocket cave that I touched her. "How about you, my little friend? Nothing to say?"

She stirred under my hand so I knew she was fine. Reserving judgment.

By the time we got back downstairs, Jilly had relaxed considerably. She didn't have to make much effort here. Instead, she chatted easily with the Hulls about granite counters, premium appliances and even favorite recipes.

No one noticed I didn't participate in the conversation. And no one noticed when I slipped out the back door with Keats and Percy.

I stood on the porch and surveyed the Hulls' domain. There was no denying that they were good candidates for a Mafia dog. They were homebodies, the home itself was roomy, and the yard was huge. A dog would have a cushy life here.

Keats offered disparaging commentary about dogs who liked cushy lives. He was annoyed to be here when he could be supervising the building of a bird coop in Maud's backyard. Edna was making Kestra do most of the work, but Olive was helping. Maybe the project would bring them closer.

Leaving the porch, I made the rounds of the yard. Energy began percolating in my pocket. Millicent gave a few squeaks, and Percy and Keats moved with more purpose. Their tails went up. Something had caught their interest. It wasn't a major threat but it was definitely worth a good look around.

The landscaping was impeccable. It seemed strange that Paige would foot the bill for that, but she was trying to build her business here, or even steal business from Glennis. Going that extra mile was probably worth it, as it seemed like she had satisfied her clients.

There was no heaviness here that I could sense. No feeling of loss and old sorrow.

And yet...

There was something amiss in the yard. The dog and the cat picked up the pace and when they finished their tour, they did it again, more slowly.

On the third pass, Percy stopped beside a rundown shed. The couple had likely kept it because it was quaint. In fact, they'd surrounded it with new shrubs that became the focus of Percy's investigation.

At a certain point, he lifted his paw as if to deliver his signature move, and then lowered it again. His meow had a melancholy quality. So melancholy, in fact, that Keats spared the cat a lick. Such overt affection between them was rare indeed.

The dog mumbled something to me that didn't quite click. My best guess was that there had been trouble here at one time, but it was over now.

Jilly joined me with the young couple, and opened her arms to beckon Percy. "What's wrong with my cat baby?"

"He has an itchy trigger paw but hasn't fired," I said.

She pressed her lips together. "Ah, I see. Well, perhaps it's time for us to go pick up our costumes."

Mika and Matt Hull looked at each other, baffled.

"Don't worry," I said. "You have a lovely home and I think after what happened with Blenda Mushing, it would be even happier without those peacock feathers."

"Agreed," Mika said. "It's awful to think she may have hurt a peacock, but I truly believe she worked some magic here. The place felt dark and sad when we bought it. And now it's bright and happy."

I smiled at them. "Perhaps that's just your influence. You seem like nice people."

Matt gave me a sly smile. "Nice enough to win the rescue challenge?"

"That's not up to us, fortunately. I would never want to make big decisions like that. It's hard enough to decide what's best for the animals that end up in my care."

"We'll see you at the party later," Jilly said. "And in the corn husk maze. I could do without that little adventure."

"I love the corn maze," Matt said. "I've visited Fairfax Farm nearly every year since I was a kid."

"Sounds like you have an edge," I said, as they walked us to the truck.

He shook his head. "They change the pattern every year. Plus, they pump in fog so you can't see much. This is where we can really blow their socks off, honey. I am so stoked."

His wife shuddered and Jilly and I joined in.

"My husband would probably love it, too," Jilly said, as we followed the animals into the truck. "I hope he's working tonight."

When the truck was rolling, I said, "Oh, he will be. There was something funny about the landscaping near the shed and the police will want to take a good long look."

"Funny?" Jilly asked. "Like stray foot funny?"

"Ask him," I said, pointing to Percy on her lap.

The cat gave some swishes of his paws before he settled.

"What does that mean?" she asked.

"It means someone needs to check the landfill." I found a smile for her as I gunned it to the costume rental. "But it won't be us, Princess."

CHAPTER EIGHTEEN

Jilly hadn't been wrong about missing all the best options at the costume rental store. There probably hadn't been many to begin with as demand in the region would normally be low. But the big party at the legion hall hosted by the Thistledown mayor had brought out the Halloween spirit in everyone.

My best friend was pouting under the head of a green lizard. I didn't need to see the pout to know it was there. Even if we hadn't agreed in advance to keep a distance to prevent partygoers from guessing our identity, I was sure she'd have given me the cold shoulder. In this case quite literally, as she turned her back on me while dragging a long heavy tail around. Olive Redding, dressed as Snow White, tried to help but tripped over Jilly's tail and fell flat on her face. She rolled over and stared at the ceiling, and I got the sense she was tempted to stay down. Life had been hard on her recently and now her legs were bound in a lot of stiff fabric.

Jilly tried to maneuver around to offer a claw to help Olive get up but it turned into such an awkward display that people fell back, laughing. I wanted to go over and help them both but couldn't give up my anonymity. Nor could our other friends, who were mostly well disguised themselves.

As it turned out, Olive wasn't down long before a man in a trench coat and fedora came to her aid. It was Nigel Byrd, who appeared to be in the role of Rick Blaine from Casablanca. The costume was decidedly low effort and that would cost him points with Cori Hogan, but the romance wasn't lost on me when he slipped his hands under Olive's armpits, lifted her easily to her feet, and sent her on her way with her lizard escort.

He got bonus points for not staring into the corner I'd staked out. Many men, including young Officer Wiebe, could not be given the same credit.

I felt completely naked.

I was about half-naked.

With the costume racks empty, the only option available to me had been Wonder Woman's red, gold and blue outfit. If the weather were warmer, that would have been gone, too. Plenty of women liked to dress in scanty attire for Halloween. I was not one of them. As someone who felt most at home in overalls, attending a party in what basically amounted to a fancy bathing suit made me feel exposed, while simultaneously shielding my identity. A black wig of flowing curls covered my hair, while a painted mask concealed most of my face. Red lipstick completed the transition from Farmer Ivy to unrecognizable superhero sleuth.

The costume itself was extremely uncomfortable. Though too big for Jilly, it was about a half size too small for me. On the bright side, the strapless one piece was tight enough to stay up and the boots were mercifully flat. I could probably run in this getup if the need arose but it wasn't meant for trick-or-treating. The point was to work the crowd in disguise and try to figure out what people knew about the bones in Olive Redding's back yard, and possibly the Hulls', as well. In a community like this, someone always knew something that may lead to another thing. The police would follow the breadcrumbs eventually, but Wonder Woman might be able to get there first.

On a normal Halloween, it bothered me that costumes allowed people to let down their guard but I was hoping it would work in my favor this time. There was a good chance people who didn't know me well wouldn't recognize me. In fact, Edna and Gertie walked right past me, no doubt convinced that I was too smart and modest to be showing so much skin on a cool night. How wrong they were.

The usual giveaways had been temporarily given away. I'd reluctantly surrendered Keats' leash to Maud Gentry, who had Frost with her as well. Annie still didn't like crowds, so she'd stayed home with Wendel Barrick, the Merriweathers and the new peacock. Louisa had handed her cat, Fanny, off to Zoe, so that she could keep a close eye on Percy, who was in a carrier. We didn't trust the cat not to "out" Jilly and me, but we also wanted him to be with us in the corn maze later.

That left me with Millicent, who was in a new carrier—a tiny, ventilated purse that had been spray-painted gold and was now sitting on the opposite hip to Wonder Woman's lasso of truth. It was on a strap that allowed it to be moved as needed to protect the mouse. It surprised me that she wanted to attend the party, but she seemed determined to get the most out of her Halloween adventure and refused to stay in the luxurious cage Maud had found.

Keats wasn't happy to be separated from me, but he was sticking with the plan. Maud, Louisa and Zoe had dressed as the Brontë sisters, in period frocks. They didn't bother with masks as the pets would expose their identities anyway.

Meanwhile, Gertie and Edna had played against type in dressing up as "classic" old ladies, in frumpy dresses, kerchiefs, wrinkled masks and canes. They hobbled around the room, ready to throw off their trappings and deliver a beatdown if needed.

It wouldn't be needed.

The point of the party was to auction off donated antiques to raise money for rescue. This strategy had worked well for the Mafia on several occasions. Those able to resist the manipulations of the

Langman sisters were often happy enough to part with treasures to help animals. The only reason the Langmans themselves were not here was that my sisters and Mom had concocted an elaborate ruse back home. With help from Dottie Bridges, the librarian, they'd leaked information about a new stash of treasure at an outpost high in the hills. Kaye and Heddy could never pass up first dibs on something like that, and they'd driven off with Poppy tailing them.

Bridget and Cori worked with Thelma behind a screen to organize the donations. Often at such events, potential buyers had a chance to view the wares first to drive a frenzy of bidding. With only Officer Wiebe in attendance, organizers had gone for a more restrained approach. Asher had taken the harder job of coordinating a search in the Hulls' yard and Kellan was on a call in a neighboring town. Judging by the glazed look in the young couple's eyes, the fun had gone out of the evening, but they were here, dressed as twin beagles and clearly determined to carry on with the competition. I hoped Percy's itchy trigger paw made the disruption of their fresh landscaping worthwhile.

I stayed in my corner, which offered a good vantage point to view the crowd. If I'd had Keats and Percy for company, and a nice warm coat, I would have been well entertained. It seemed like most of the town's population had come out and the majority had made some effort to find a costume. The mayor was in the topcoat and tails of a circus ringmaster, which was so on the nose I found myself liking him even before we'd officially met. The auction and the corn maze run to follow could very well devolve into a circus.

Three witches had gathered in front of the stage. All looked so similar in their fluttering black gowns, heavy green makeup and steepled hats that it took me a few moments to figure out their identities. Their voices and gestures finally gave them away. Faige Ogilvy had sprinkled fake warts with a liberal hand, whereas Glennis Redding had none at all. Blenda Mushing had a lightning bolt scar down one cheek. I wasn't too surprised about the two real estate agents dressing alike, as Paige imitated Glennis on a regular day. Blenda's costume was unexpected. She had seemed a little touchy about witches when I visited her store and probably hadn't developed a sense of humor overnight. Perhaps the three women were closer than I'd realized. The inner workings of the Thistledown coven were still relatively new to me.

Cori Hogan came out from behind the screen and I had to muffle a laugh with one of my Wonder Woman wrist cuffs. The tiny trainer had dressed as a black bird with faux feather wings strapped to each arm that each bore a patch of neon orange. I'd never told her that's how I saw her, so either she was as intuitive as Janelle or she was more self-aware than she liked to let on. The gloves didn't get turfed for the sake of the costume, but tonight's version appeared to be black rubber for a better grip. The middle fingers were wrapped in orange hazard tape.

Close on Cori's wings was Bridget, dressed as a jester, complete with harlequin makeup. Beau was at her side wearing a matching bandana. That was the worst she would do to her dignified dog, who was, after all, the true judge of the rescue competition.

And Thelma... Well, she took the crown, quite literally, being thoroughly disguised as Queen Elizabeth I. Her wig under the crown was red, her white makeup thick and her dress looked rich and heavy. Hanging from her waist was a long golden scepter that would also serve as her cane if she needed it. I might not have known it was her, but for the classic librarian pucker. I suspected someone had offended her and it probably involved the items on the sterling silver tray she carried out.

The mayor stepped into a circle drawn on the makeshift stage and bowed deeply to the crowd. After a typically political introduction, calling attention to Thistledown's increasing profile, he responded to a poke from Thelma's scepter and got the auction going.

A Tiffany lamp set things off to a great start with a lively bidding war among the three witches and some well-heeled older locals. The lamp went to Glennis, and her husband, who wasn't in costume, claimed it for her.

Next up was a sterling silver tea set and the same bidders threw up their hands in a flurry of bids. Glennis landed this prize, too, although her smirk made me wonder if she'd only competed to take it from Paige.

A shiver ran through me as Cori carried out a creepy doll that was very similar to the one in Olive's home and the original one haunting my memories. To my surprise, another flurry of bids between the three women ensued, and the doll ultimately ended up in Blenda's clutches.

Was it a coincidence that the three had such an ardent interest in antiques? I couldn't get close enough to see if they had the gleam in their eyes of the crazed collector. That obsession drove the Langmans to do unethical things, but plenty of people loved antiques in a more balanced way.

After that came a series of lesser items, at least judging by the witches who stopped bidding. Smiles lit up the room as everyone who wanted something got it.

While the tension in the room went down, it escalated in my glammed-up fanny pack. Millicent had been as quiet as the proverbial mouse but something got her flustered now.

Feeling fur brush against my bare knee, I figured out why. Fanny, Louisa Gentry's pretty gray cat, had escaped Zoe to pay a visit. At first, I thought the mouse had attracted her attention, but then I noticed a square of paper tucked into her collar.

Unfolding the note, I recognized Thelma's handwriting. "Anonymous donation," it said. Underneath she'd drawn a scrolly E and O.

Eliza Ormiston.

Whatever was coming up next must have belonged to Vikki Tickle's sister. Had Vikki donated anonymously? Had someone stolen the donation from Olive Redding's house? Thelma wanted me to take action.

I would need to leave my corner and deliver the message in person.

"Vikki," I whispered, coming up behind the old woman. She was dressed as Raggedy Ann, but a lock of blue hair had slipped out of her wig.

"Wonder Woman," she said. "Do I know you?"

I nodded. "Code word, 'postcards.'"

"Got it. What's wrong?"

Leaning in close, I said, "I have it on good authority that an item belonging to your sister is going up for auction. Did you donate?"

"Of course not." She sounded horrified. "I'd never give something of Eliza's away."

"Then it must have been stolen from your childhood home and should rightly belong to you. Should we speak to the mayor?"

Vikki flicked her red pigtails from side to side. "Let's let this play out. Leave it to me."

The mayor used his white gloves to display a hand mirror, brush and comb, all with tarnished silver frames, and a strange accessory that had two spikes about five or six inches long.

"Bun prong," Vikki whispered. "There was a pair, engraved. Eliza did my hair once and I remember how they hurt."

"The other one may still be at the house," I said. "I bet these things were in the attic." The idea came from the tiny whirling dervish in my fanny pack. Millicent was worked up, and since Fanny had faded into the crowd, it didn't seem related to the cat.

The mayor started taking bids and hands flew into the air. Eight or nine people tried to win the purloined items. Queen Thelma looked across the crowd at me and puckered harder. I flicked up my thumb to tell her we had it under control, although I had no idea if that was true.

Glennis, Paige and Blenda were driving the price up fast. Their green-gloved hands flew as they outbid each other.

"Vultures," Vikki muttered. "Bad as the Langmans."

"We need to do something." Millicent was increasingly distressed, although I was confident only I could hear her cheeps. The room was very loud.

"Watch and wait." Vikki calmly adjusted her wig. "If you're patient, the trash eventually takes itself out."

Impatience was one of my bigger shortcomings. "I should get Officer Wiebe. That's stolen property."

Vikki shook her wig again, revealing more blue and green tendrils. "I want to see how high they'll go."

The bidding slowed as the price tipped over a thousand dollars. Then the bids crept up in smaller increments. But as the bids got lower, the voices got louder. Paige eventually dropped out, leaving Glennis and Blenda lobbing bids at each other. The gap in between got longer and finally the mayor said, "Going... Going..."

"Two thousand," Vikki shouted.

"Do I hear two thousand and fifty?" the mayor asked.

"Three thousand," Glennis called out.

"Thirty-five hundred," Blenda countered.

Finally, someone in the crowd shouted, "Five thousand."

It was Heddy Langman. Somehow she'd evaded Poppy and made it down here, perhaps to scoop these very items.

The mayor looked in our direction. "Raggedy Ann? What say you?"

"Two thousand," Vikki repeated. "Consider it a donation to rescue, but that set belongs to me fair and square. It's engraved with my sister's initials. As I'm her only living relative, I'd be very surprised if there's a legal record of sale for it."

There was a kerfuffle among the witches, and Heddy shouted objections.

The mayor's smile evaporated and he made a snap decision. "We withdraw this item pending further investigation."

After that, the auction went on with less drama. Glennis, Paige and Blenda stepped back from the podium, either because nothing else interested them or they didn't want to draw the mayor's attention.

Everyone stayed focused, no doubt hoping for another bombshell, and I used the distraction to move around unnoticed. Well, Officer Wiebe noticed me, but again for the wrong reasons. I could hardly blame him. At least the goose bumps on my arms and legs had subsided as the heat went up in the room.

The conversations I overheard were nothing unexpected. People assumed the bones in the pumpkin patch had been Eliza Ormiston's and thus drove up the value of her belongings. It stirred a little nausea in my empty stomach and I wished I'd taken time to eat more than chocolate apple cake and fudge at the fair. Wonder Woman probably lived on more than sweets and her likeness deserved better. Surprisingly, the news that there were two bodies didn't seem widely known. Halloween and the rescue event had shorted out the rumor mill.

Something made me look across the room to where Maud was standing with the dogs. Keats raised his white paw in a point and Frost immediately followed suit.

"A double point, Millicent," I said. "We're missing some action."

Weaving faster through the crowd in the direction the dogs indicated, I ended up behind the stage. The partitions shielded me from two women arguing but I knew their voices and their heated tone made me wish I had my phone to record them.

"We had an agreement," Paige Ogilvy said.

"*You* had an agreement," Blenda Mushing replied. "I said I was still thinking about it."

"You did not. We shook hands. That's a gentleman's agreement."

"Look, we're not friends and in situations like this, it's every gentleman for herself. The stakes changed."

There was a long pause and then Paige said, "You'll regret this."

"Oh? How so?"

The next pause, unfortunately, was filled with paws—busy little ones vibrating against my hip. Millicent was demanding my attention and I had to assume she wanted me to move away from the warring women.

Sighing, I slipped around another partition only to find another pair arguing, albeit in hushed tones. It was Glennis Redding and her husband.

"This has got to stop, honey," he said. "I'm getting worried."

"It's the last time," she said. "The last one. I promise."

He shook his head and I wished Glennis could see him through Wonder Woman's eyes. This man loved her but she'd pushed him to the end of his tether. If she didn't stop doing whatever was upsetting him, she would lose what I'd heard was a long marriage.

"You'll retire?" he said. "Because that's what I need."

"I don't want to retire." Glennis sounded whiny. "My family works right up to the end. You know that."

"It's time to break with family tradition," he said. "You're stressed all the time now. Just settle with Paige and call it done. Let her take over and we'll head south and stick our toes in the sand."

Now I wished he could see his wife through Wonder Woman's eyes. Glennis would never be happy in a lounge chair by the sea. After all these years, they were on the brink of disaster.

"It's not just about Paige," she said. "It's also that witch, who—"

If only I hadn't accidentally leaned into the wall and nearly squished Millicent. Her indignant squeak cut the couple's conversation short, but I was able to slip away before they noticed. At least I hoped so. This costume was extremely hard to hide but the light was low in the back of the legion hall.

"No offense, Millicent," I said, "but I really miss my dog."

Her chittering sounded a little saucy. Perhaps she missed the peace of attic life, where no one was jostling her around or squishing her.

A woman dressed as a fat and fluffy black cat came up to me. "I heard that, Ivy. Totally gave yourself away talking to your fanny pack and giving it a pat."

I glared at Kestra, knowing the impact was diminished by my mask. "Go away. I'm incognito."

"Your secret is safe with me. But I thought you'd want to know that Paige is hassling Olive. I'd handle it alone, but you warned me earlier about the perils of being a hothead."

"Hotheads unite," I said. "Lead the way."

As we approached Olive and Jilly, her lizard protector, Keats jerked the leash out of Maud's hand and joined me. When my fingers touched his head, a welcome warmth flooded through me. Wonder Woman may have superpowers, but a hobby farmer wearing plastic wrist cuffs needed a dog to fill the gaps.

"What's going on?" Kestra asked, stepping in front of her sister.

Paige, the witch with the warts, brushed the younger Redding aside. "I'm counseling my client to negotiate with the Sprockets and settle."

"I don't want to settle," Olive said. "There was a body in the garden, Paige. Yesterday, you were outraged on my account."

Paige's smile looked oddly yellow with the green makeup. "I did more research and realized you're never going to find a property like that for the price in hill country."

"That's the point," Olive said. "I don't want a property like that anymore. I wouldn't have bought it in the first place if I'd realized there'd been a murder there."

"You don't know that happened. And if you want to live in this community, it's important to be reasonable. To seem like a team player."

Olive pulled up her mask and stared. "That's what it takes to be a team player here?"

The lizard signaled to me. Normally Jilly would be the one trying to smooth the waters, but the heavy plastic costume must be weighing down her charm.

"Paige," I said, moving in with Keats. "This isn't the time or place for a business conversation."

She turned on me. "What do you know about etiquette, Wonder Woman? Put some clothes on. That costume is indecent."

I was torn between being amused and offended, but Keats came down on the side of indignation and delivered a nip to Paige's calf.

"I know a good lawyer," someone said. "And that's what Olive needs."

Turning, we saw Nigel Byrd. Maybe he hadn't blown it out of the park with his costume but there was a lot to be said for the quiet hero type.

"We don't need a lawyer to settle this like adults," Paige said.

Nigel pulled up the collar of his trench coat. "There's nothing to settle before the police finish their investigation. And then lawyers can take over." He turned to Olive. "How does that sound?"

Olive just nodded but a muffled voice from inside the lizard costume told Paige to leave. The language was ruder than I was used to hearing from my tactful best friend, but you never knew what to expect from a lizard.

CHAPTER NINETEEN

Fairfax Farm was everything I initially thought I was buying in a hobby farm. It was small and quaint, with just a few friendly animals. The goats were as mild-mannered as sheep and the sheep so bland as to seem artificial. Naturally, their pig was delightful, too. It had a heart-shaped gray splotch on its side and invited scratches from anyone who leaned over the pen.

Keats mumbled a wakeup call: boring.

These animals had likely led easy lives from their first breath, whereas nearly all of mine came from hardship. I may have had a romanticized view of my future when Hannah Pemberton reached out, but I had given up on "easy" the day I chased Keats' criminal owner with a skull in my handbag.

If I'd wanted a boring life, I would still be in a corporate tower in human resources. Downsizing people and breaking their hearts wasn't doing it for me, however. I wanted to rescue them, too.

"Hey, Wonder Woman," Cori called. "Time to put those superpowers to work. I thought you were all about saving lives."

Keats gave a pant-laugh and I joined in. "It's just a corn maze, Cori. But I do agree winning the right dog could save someone's life."

Tonight was our last chance to get Olive and Kestra across the finish line in the rescue competition. All of the contestants were being sent into the corn maze at intervals and would be scored on the time it took to get through, as well as their grace under pressure. The latter was to be determined by their escort. Jilly was going in first with Olive. Edna had the Hulls and Gertie another couple. Zoe was assigned Nigel Byrd, and Louisa a pair of senior citizen sisters. The last contestant, another senior, took one look at the maze and dropped out of the competition, despite having Bridget as her escort. I didn't really blame her. The amount of fog they were pumping in was completely unnecessary. Anyone could trip and fall.

Cori walked Jilly and Olive to the starting point and I followed with Kestra. "Just get in and get out," she said, gloves flashing. "I ran it alone earlier in seven minutes."

"In a lizard costume?" Jilly's voice was muffled, but her snarky tone translated perfectly. "In the dark?"

"It'll be fun," Cori said. "There are two of you working together. But no phones or flashlights, and Percy stays behind. He'd give you an unfair advantage."

The lizard claw reached out and grabbed one of Cori's wings. "No Percy, no Jilly. I did not sign on for something like this, Cori Hogan."

There was a sassy flutter of orange-fingered gloves. "Fine. But if someone complains, it's on you."

Jilly delivered a similar gesture, only with green plastic claws. "Hit it, Olive."

Cori made Kestra and me wait to the very end, when all the other contestants were in the maze. "You're going to insist on taking Keats," she said. "I can feel it. Someone's all needy."

It was true. The fog and the chill made me so uneasy I would have appreciated taking a bonus dog, too. Maud was waiting among other spectators with Frost and Fanny, Lou's cat. An utter waste of a great dog's skills and energy. The way Frost strained on her leash told me she agreed.

I crossed my arms, making plastic wrist cuffs clatter. "You'd be needy, too, if you were about to run a prickly maze in a bathing suit."

"Why didn't you get a cape?" Cori asked. "Wonder Woman wore one for big occasions, no?"

"The store didn't have one. But a cape probably would have been more of a hindrance," I said. "If we move fast enough, I can stay warm."

Kestra crouched at the maze entrance like a racer. "Let's kill it."

Cori clicked the timer and we were off. The cornrows were wide enough to walk side by side but the tall, dried stalks scraped my skin, snagged my costume and grabbed at my wig. I moved Millicent around to sit in front of me so she didn't get jostled too much. Every step felt dangerous because of limited visibility. The stalks were about 10 feet high and had a closed-in feeling. There were four identical lights on poles—one in each corner of the maze—casting a weak, yellowy glow over the area. Filtered through fog, it was almost worse than nothing at all. At least we didn't need to worry about fake zombies or giant spiders. Cori had been disappointed when town officials nixed that plan, but if someone had a heart attack, there was no local health center. That could bring the wrong sort of press.

It was just a long, dark and twisty path, and aside from tripping, the only real threat was my own imagination.

"Don't worry," I told Kestra. "Slow and steady."

"I'm not worried. Are you worried?"

I was worried. My imagination was always ready to add spice to strange situations, and this was a new story. "Glad Halloween is almost over," I said.

"Not long till Thanksgiving. Holidays come hard and fast now. I love it."

I laughed. "I'm more selective, but I love most of them, too. Especially the food. We just need to get through this."

"We just need to *enjoy* this," Kess said. "It's all about attitude."

She was right. I wasn't usually this negative. It sounded like my friends were caught in the same trap. Far ahead, there was cackling and complaining, including a loud, "Dagnabit."

"One more dead end and I'm going right through a corn wall," Gertie said. "I only have a few years left on the planet and I don't plan on spending them stuck in here."

"Age is just a number, old friend," Edna bellowed, joining Gertie in a witchy cackle.

"They're pretty cool," Kess said. "Scary, but cool."

"Don't forget funny. They're exactly what I want as the buffer we discussed earlier." Keats mumbled a suggestion. "Along with the perfect dog."

Kestra was pushing the pace while I lagged. "Can we win this?" she asked.

"Not without Keats taking over. Edna and Gertie are superb navigators and they're struggling. Do you want to win fairly or cheat?"

I honestly figured she'd say "cheat," but she surprised me. "Fair and square. I just want to do my best. That's what Gran taught me." She turned a cornrow corner and sighed. "For all the good it's done."

"It'll pay off when you least expect it." I rested my fingers on Keats' head. The prickle of fur between his ears told me he was uneasy but I didn't want to spook Kess. She really was in it to win it, forging ahead of me and making bold decisions on the turns. "Careful. It feels like we're going back where we came."

She shook her head, which was still covered in the black fuzzy hood of her cat costume. "I think I've got it."

"Got what?"

There was just enough light to see her clawed mitten point upward. "Navigation. I've sat through a ton of lectures at Howler Hall. Most of them will never be useful but the astronomy series just came in handy. I know where we're supposed to come out and I can get us there."

Keats mumbled a "knock yourself out" and we let her run the show. She reminded me of a kid's toy wound up too tight.

"How many coffees have you had?" I asked.

Her laugh was slightly manic. "Too many. And too much sugar. I regretted the candy apple then, but now it's turned into fuel."

Put me in a holiday sweater and we would basically be twins.

Still ahead of me, she called back, "What did you make of that auction? There's something weird going on with those ladies."

"Quiet. You know how sound carries. I can still hear Edna cursing."

"I'm just saying. I saw Glennis and Paige arguing in a corner and next thing you know Paige was twisting Olive's arm into giving up the fight on the house."

"They were probably arguing over the auction. It was strangely competitive, but I've seen that happen before with antiques."

There was a rustle down a row to our right. "This way," Kess said, more quietly. "Leave them in the dust."

We moved on quickly past Gertie and the couple she was escorting. That happened again with other contestants. If Kestra was right about her navigation, we'd be out of here in no time and have to go back to collect the others.

She was staring up at the stars when I heard the first strange sound.

"What was that?" I whispered.

"What was what?" She was so intent on her task that she didn't hear it.

I'd actually directed my question at Keats, anyway, and he mumbled a warning.

"What did he say?" Kestra asked. "It didn't sound encouraging."

"No, it did not. I think we might be running into a spot of trouble."

As it turned out, a spot of trouble was running into *us*.

CHAPTER TWENTY

The pig with the heart-shaped gray splotch on its side wasn't nearly as nice as it had seemed in its pen an hour ago. Now loose in the maze, it was angry. Probably more afraid than angry, but emotions blended sometimes and they had no place to go in this maze. Like us, the pig was sticking to the carved out rows when it could easily have plunged through the stalks and run to freedom.

"Whoa," Kestra said, jumping aside as it charged. "I did not see that coming."

There was too little light and too much fog to see much of anything, but my ears didn't let me down. "He's circling back. And he's not happy."

Kestra and I scattered. She dashed into one row and I another, snapping my fingers for Keats. It wasn't the right setting to play the herding hero. I knew all too well what it felt like to be squished under a runaway pig.

We ran down a row, turned a corner and then a few more. I did my best to cushion the impact for the mouse in her gold case.

"Cori!" I called out, remembering how voices carried. "Everyone! The pig is loose in the maze. Be careful."

In no time at all, I was completely disoriented. Fear made my heart pound, even though I knew I could plunge through the rows if necessary. The trap was probably more mental than physical, but it sure felt real.

"It's just a pig," I said aloud. "Nothing we haven't faced before."

Keats mumbled something that didn't sound too positive. He wasn't in control of the situation and he didn't like that. Under better circumstances, herding a pig was hard enough. In these conditions, it would be nearly impossible.

"Someone's going to get hurt," I said. "Who would do this? Not Cori. She'd never put a pig in peril."

I tried a few more twists and turns in the maze, sensing that rather than moving out, I was going deeper into its heart. Keats was doing his best to shuttle me along but he changed his mind on the route twice. His growl was frustrated and perhaps slightly confused, making me wonder if a pig was the only problem we had to worry about. Finally, I just stopped moving. Flailing around wasn't helping. Maybe we could strategize our way out.

We stood for a moment and despite many others being stuck in this maze with me, it was oddly quiet. Maybe the corn stalks were absorbing sound, or maybe people were trying to keep the pig from knowing their location. Either way, I suddenly felt very much alone in the Halloween heart of darkness. The horror. The horror.

Keats gave my bare knee a poke that probably would have been a nip if he wasn't worried I'd tip over into crazy and start randomly thrashing around.

"Yeah, I know. We've faced worse. It's not like there's a sociopath out here." I did a full turn. "Is it weird that I'd rather face a deranged human than an angry pig? Sometimes you can reason with the human. Never the pig."

Staring up at the sky, I wished I'd taken the time to learn to navigate by the stars, too. Without my phone and GPS, I could get lost in my own pastures. The full moon had hoisted itself over the edge of the tall corn and started casting a pale glow that only seemed to create more shadows. A bat flew overhead. Then another. Soon there were half a dozen moving in a small circle. A shiver ran down my spine.

"Just bats crossing the full moon on Halloween," I muttered. "Nothing creepy about that at all."

A squeak from the golden mouse case reminded me of my passenger. She hadn't made a sound—or at least one I could hear—as I ran through the rows. Now she wanted attention.

She cheeped again and it seemed like the bats circled in closer. "Other way, Millicent. Other way. We don't want bats stuck in here with us."

The bats fluttered out of sight and I let out a long breath. While a pig could do more harm, Keats couldn't do much to fend off six flying critters if they decided to whack me around in tight confines.

"Good. They've moved on." I stood on tiptoe. "Oops! They're back."

They repeated the same flight pattern until I realized it *was* a flight pattern.

"Do they want us to follow them?" The question was directed at Keats but it was Millicent who answered with a chittering sound. In my head, those little noises arranged themselves into a sentence: "Of course, silly."

It was as good a strategy as any. "Keats, let's follow the bats. They've got an aerial view and I doubt we'll be any worse off."

His next mumble didn't sound convinced, but it did sound resigned. My dog was discouraged. He didn't meet many animals he couldn't herd or at least influence. Bats were certainly among them.

The bats swirled in a small cloud above us and it was hard to intuit exactly where they wanted me to go. But the trend was definitely in one direction, so I kept moving that way.

"We must be nearly out of here," I said. "The whole thing is forty acres. I feel like we've covered forty miles already, but we've probably backtracked a few times."

Millicent kept up a steady cheeping, almost birdlike in its intensity and regularity. It felt like a tiny anvil banging on my brain.

"If you're trying to tell me something, my little friend, I'm missing the point. I followed your bat buddies and where are we now?"

The straight rows gradually transitioned into a circular route. My stomach twisted into a hard knot as I remembered people talking about the maze earlier. Someone had mentioned a spiral carved right in the center of it.

In other words, we were as far from "out" as possible. Exactly where we *didn't* want to be.

Only I wasn't driving.

Keats wasn't driving.

And a bloodcurdling shriek told me someone had reached the middle first.

CHAPTER TWENTY-ONE

The center of the corn maze was a cleared circle about five yards in diameter. A line of short solar lights marked the perimeter and added a warm glow to the cool rays of the moon.

That was about all that was warm here, and a tremor passed through me that had nothing to do with the chilly breeze brushing my bare arms and legs. The owners had set up a display guaranteed to terrify youngsters and probably most adults. Maybe I should have listened to Cori about the adult diaper, although it would have been harder to hide in this costume.

Two stuffed witches had been arranged in a murderous tableau. One lay on the ground beside a pool of fake blood that glittered slightly on the soil. The other was bent over the prone body holding a witchy weapon of some sort. It looked like a tuning fork, but probably had magical significance. I made it a point not to know much about witches. If they did exist, I was sure they wouldn't be wearing fluttering black dresses and steepled hats. Too cliché.

Keats gave a low, deep growl that Millicent matched with a high, sharp squeak.

"It's just a fake, Keats. Like the body in the library parking lot. Remember?"

He shot a bolt of eerie blue eye at me. As if he would forget. He had known that was a prank and enjoyed it. There was no enjoyment in his stance now. He was thoroughly puffed and his eyeteeth gleamed in the solar lights.

It was an uncharacteristic overreaction. I could only assume a true threat lurked nearby, perhaps even more pressing than a stray pig.

"What's going on?" My voice fell to a whisper and I took a few steps toward the witch tableau.

That's when I saw something had changed. The witch on the ground hadn't moved, but the one bending over her had. In fact, she was moving now, straightening with slow, jerky motions.

Ugh. It was automated, too.

As if on cue, a fog machine pumped out a great puff that rolled around in a heavy cloud that mostly shrouded the witch on the ground. I wouldn't want to be sucking in those chemicals if I were her. She had the easier job but it came with hazards.

Halloween was ridiculously over the top these days. If it continued this way, I would advocate with Kellan to boycott it for our future children. There was enough to traumatize them in this world.

After the mobile witch reached the upright position, her arm dropped and the tuning fork fell to her side. A solar light was positioned just right to catch the metal in its beam and that's when I gasped. It wasn't a tuning fork at all.

It was a bun prong.

A bun prong that looked very similar to the antique hair accessory in Eliza Ormiston's engraved collection.

"Okay, well, that's just tacky." My voice got louder with indignation. "Vikki said there was a bun prong missing from the auction. They used it in their stupid display out here? I'm lodging a formal complaint. And I'm also taking that one back to Vikki Tickle, where it belongs."

Keats gave me a warning grumble but I was angry and determined. I started walking and he ran ahead to turn me around. If I'd been wearing a more cumbersome costume, he might have succeeded. Instead, I dodged around him easily and all he got for his nip was a mouthful of costume boot.

I crossed the last couple of yards, and probably didn't even take a breath before reaching out to grab the bun prong.

My fingers brushed against the faux witch's hand and I gasped again.

It was warm.

"YOU'RE ACTORS," I said. "Listen, give me that thing right now or my dog will have you for a late-night snack."

The actor witch released the fork without the slightest resistance and I felt a sticky dampness on my hand. Looking down, I saw fake blood on my fingers. They'd gone all out for this. I supposed it was great marketing for the farm and even the town.

Since I hadn't had a heart attack.

Yet.

Hardheaded hotheads were probably on the "most likely" list for cardiac episodes.

"Look, I'm not easily offended, but you've crossed a line here," I said. "It's so incredibly tasteless that I'll be taking it up with whoever hired you. A name, please and thank you."

Keats had inserted himself between me and the witches and was pressing me back. Even Wonder Woman had to succumb to a stubborn sheepdog. But that didn't stop my voice from rising.

"Hey, look at me," I called. "I want to know who paid you to do this."

"No one."

The two words were mere puffs of air and nearly unintelligible. If she spoke a little louder, I suspected I'd recognize the voice.

"This is a volunteer gig? Then it's on you."

"Not me," she murmured.

Finally, her chin came up and I noticed a scattering of warts on the heavy green makeup.

"Paige? Is that you?" She didn't answer so I continued. "Are you really so hard up for cash you'd participate in something like this? Shameless."

I started to turn away, but this time the dog turned me back.

Paige Ogilvy was still frozen in position so I looked down instead. The heavy fog shifted and left my sightline clear.

The witch on the ground had a lightning bolt on her cheek. She was staring up at the moonlit sky, and the ever-circling bats, with pale blue eyes. The palest I'd ever seen. And they were unblinking.

Blenda Mushing sure knew how to strike a pose.

Now, Keats started moving me away. I kept staring at Blenda staring.

Resisting the dog's relentless push, I stopped walking. I was determined to see Blenda blink.

It didn't happen.

What *did* happen is that something hit my legs from behind, suddenly and hard. My knees buckled and I fell over backward.

CHAPTER TWENTY-TWO

If I'd been able to read the stars overhead they would have spelled out tragedy, with fluttering bats as punctuation.

Blenda Mushing was dead and Paige Ogilvy had stabbed her with a hair accessory.

Since I was now in possession of the murder weapon, the bigger problem was the living, breathing murder weapon that knocked me over. There was a grunt and a squeal further down the corn maze spiral. Would the rogue pig come back for more, or find a new victim?

At least I had fallen on my back while the fanny pack was twisted to the front. Otherwise, it could have ended very badly for the mouse and my conscience.

"Millicent, you okay?" I sat up, while holding the burr prong and shielding the mouse.

A chirp told me she was, but it sounded like she was wearying of this game.

"Yeah, me too." I struggled to maneuver onto my knees. "Keats? Where are you?"

The pig made up his mind and came back into the center of the labyrinth with my dog in pursuit. The animals ran around the perimeter and the two moving bodies made the lights seem to flicker. That was the first time I noticed the other exit. Would Paige make a run for it?

"Help!" I yelled. "I've got a 911 in the middle of the maze. I repeat, 911!"

A fluffy black cat in human form was the first to reach me. "Ivy, you okay?"

"Stay where you are, Kess," I said. "We've got a situation here."

"Keats has the pig cornered. Well, there are no corners. That's the problem."

"It's not the only problem, trust me."

"Wait, what?" Her voice spiked. "There are witches. He's trapped the pig with the witches."

"Help me up, Kess. Fast. Use my elbow. Whatever you do, don't touch the murder weapon."

"The... *what?* Did you hit your head again?"

"Ivy!" The voice was muffled, but I recognized it as that of my best friend. Percy raced into the circle, cut in front of Keats and delivered his verdict on Blenda with a flourish of orange paws. That saved me from spelling it out for Jilly myself.

The cat was soon stranded with the victim, because a blaze of brown-and-white fur joined Keats, and Frost began circling the clearing in the opposite direction. If pig or Paige had a notion to run, they didn't stand a chance.

Cori reached us next, coming in from the other entrance. One wing was gone and the other askew. Digesting at least part of the scenario, she pulled a phone from her pocket and called 911.

I had rarely been more grateful for modern technology. How had I ever survived without a cell phone?

After that, the dogs weren't the only blur.

Cori ripped off her other wing and charged in among the dogs with Bridget, still bright in her jester costume. Edna was shedding old lady attire as she ran into the circle. The Hulls dropped back and hugged each other, still adorable as twin beagles.

"Wonder Woman! Wake up, dagnabit. Toss me your magic lasso."

In all the hubbub I'd forgotten that part of my costume, hanging on my hip. Even if I'd remembered it, I wouldn't have been able to snare a pig.

Turns out that wasn't the plan, anyway. Cori let the two dogs herd the pig out of the maze and followed the animals with Bridget. That left Edna to tie up Paige and ease her to the ground. The warty witch turned her back on the prone body and stared into the darkness of the tall stalks.

It was the easiest takedown ever. No resistance. No signature ear-ripping or feline scalp massage. The murderer remained completely silent, despite her leg being bent in what must be an uncomfortable position.

"What just happened?" Olive asked, walking closer to the body and then letting Edna nudge her quite firmly back to the rest of us. Zoe and Nigel Byrd had joined us, too. Louisa and her senior contestants were still out in the maze, it seemed.

I shook my head. "No idea what went down between Paige and Blenda. To be honest, when I got here I thought it was a bit of theater put on by the farm owners. Took Keats to convince me it was real."

Gertie arrived with her contestants, assessed the situation quickly, and backed them into the corn corridor again. She beckoned to the Hulls, who scampered over. "How about I take everyone to the starting point? If I can find the starting point."

"Better stay," I said. "The police will be here soon and it will cause more confusion if they need to locate too many missing people."

This was turning into a Halloween no one in Thistledown—or their descendants—would ever forget.

Fog continued to pump out in thick clouds until Edna knelt to grope around in the corn and found both machine and switch. Instantly, the mood felt lighter and the moonlight became brighter. The bats continued to flitter around. Always six. No more, no less.

Nigel came over and bent to pick up something at my feet. When I grabbed the lasso, I'd accidentally dropped the murder weapon. Now it was not only covered in dirt, but additional fingerprints.

The cop in charge wasn't going to be happy. Good thing he couldn't fully disown me, at least while living rent free.

Edna pulled a plastic bag out of her pocket and passed it to me, and I asked Nigel to drop the weapon inside.

"What is that? he asked, staring through the clear plastic.

"A bun prong," I said.

He looked utterly perplexed. "A what?"

"Basically a double spike to hold a woman's hair in place."

No need to mention whose hair it had secured. I had learned a few things from Kellan, and also the man racing into the maze now.

"Where is she?" My brother's voice was tight and tense.

"Right here," Olive said, gesturing to the witches. "Blenda Mushing is right here."

Kestra pointed, too. "Unless you mean Paige Ogilvy. She's right there. Trying to melt into the corn stalks."

I wanted to laugh, but somehow bit it back. My brother had excellent vision and could see the two witches. What he couldn't see was his wife. At the moment, he was not a cop but a worried husband. "And Jilly's right over there," I said.

He looked around. "Where?"

"The lizard, brother."

"The—" He stopped and walked over. "Jilly? Honey, is that you?"

I didn't hear her response but it was enough to snap his cop backbone into place. All of a sudden his arms were flapping again like he was directing traffic.

"Everyone out," he called. "File out of the maze, people. Single line. Then gather in a group and do not speak." He flashed some cop arms at his colleague. "Wiebe. Keep an eye on my sister. Do NOT let her out of your sight. And call Harper, STAT."

"Honestly, young man," Edna said. "The situation is very much contained. The murderer is the meekest I have ever seen, and that is saying something."

"It's the lasso of truth," Kestra said. "Question her now and you'll find out everything you need."

Jilly finally pulled off the lizard head and hurled it high into the cornrows. "Kestra, put a lid on it. This is serious business."

"It's okay, Jilly." I joined my best friend. "Kestra scored points for coming back to save me. She thought the villain was a pig, but still... she came back."

"The villain is far worse than a pig," Olive said. "I recognize the murder weapon."

"Murder weapon?" my brother said. "Where is it?"

I pulled the plastic bag out of my pocket and handed it over. "Sorry, brother. You'll find my prints and Nigel's, as well as Paige's."

He stared at it. "In other words, it's useless."

"Get a confession," Kestra urged. "While Paige is weak."

Asher glared at her and walked away. I followed. "Sorry, Ash. It was a few minutes of mayhem, what with the loose pig and all. I thought the two witches were actors."

He pulled me into the other exit and I prepared for a barrage of harsh words. Instead, he kept his voice low. "What more do you know, Ivy? I don't get the connection between these witches and the bones in the pumpkin patch."

"I don't, either." After filling him in on what I overheard at the auction, I said, "So, you know what I know. Do I know what *you* know?"

His eyes, so much bluer than Blenda's, darted around and landed on Jilly behind me. "We got an ID, based on an engraved legion pin buried in the garden. The bodies belong to Hildy and Gunner Danner. They rented the house from the guy who bought the place from the Ormistons. Gunner was in serious debt with Alonzo Pyle, Senior. Everyone thought the Danners ran for it. Turns out someone smacked them in the head before they could."

I covered my mouth in horror and then swallowed hard. "I don't get the link to what happened tonight. Maybe there's no link at all. But if the pieces do fit together, you'll figure it out."

Keats and Frost trotted back into the clearing, shoulder to shoulder. My dog came to check on me first and after grounding myself with a short hug, I released him to escort the others back to command central.

"Officers Keats and Frost," Asher said, as Wiebe led people out of the clearing, "if you find stragglers, bring them in. Please."

Both border collies saluted with a wave of their white tail tufts before crouching and beginning the roundup. Keats was always happy to work but there was extra flair in his moves tonight as he worked with his sister. Their usual competition vanished. This was true canine partnership at its finest. Jilly borrowed a flashlight from Asher and we followed with Olive and Kestra. It was a long walk, but it felt much different now, with the light, the cat in Jilly's arms, and more human company.

Kestra watched the stars and took over the lead. Eventually, she forced her way through a high wall of corn and we found ourselves on the outside of the huge labyrinth. My breath came more easily, even though the meeting point was nowhere in sight. All we had to do was walk around the outside of the maze until we found it.

Jilly relaxed, too, and even smiled when Frost popped out of the corn wall and fell into step beside Olive. After a few minutes, my friend pointed from one sister to the other. "Most people would be in shock but you two seem to be taking this in stride."

"I'm upset," Olive said. "But I suppose a little relieved as well. While we don't know exactly what happened, I'm hoping it's a step toward the truth." She turned to look at her sister and then her fingers dropped to Frost's head. I wondered if she even realized she was drawing comfort and strength from a good dog. "I'm not fearless like Kess."

"I was mighty afraid of that pig," Kestra said. "So scared I ran and left Ivy alone. I'm ashamed about that."

"Don't be," I said. "I wasn't alone. I had Keats and Millicent. Plus the bats. If you hadn't told me to look up at the stars, I might not have noticed the flight pattern of my winged friends." I sighed. "If I'd gotten to the middle faster, maybe I could have stopped Paige."

Olive sighed, too. "I liked Paige, at least until earlier tonight. It makes me question my judgement. Again."

"Always a good practice. Jilly and I wake up every day and remind each other to question our judgement."

My best friend finally laughed. "It does help keep us sane."

Kestra tugged on Olive's sleeve. "Midnight hide and seek. That's why we're okay now."

Olive thought about that for a second and then smiled. "Probably. Never been more terrified in my life than running around Howler Hall at night. There are so many secret rooms and cubbyholes."

"Remember when we couldn't find Allie? She fell asleep in a locker and didn't come out till morning." She continued over Olive's laughter. "There was always that horrible moment when someone jumped out at you and screeched. Especially the boys."

"I guess that's why we're not as flustered as you'd expect," Olive said. "We were training for this in childhood."

"No bodies or bloodshed, though," Kestra added. "New element we could do without."

Jilly and I dropped back and the sisters gravitated toward each other. Finally, Olive looped her arm through Kestra's. "It was fun."

"Fun?" Jilly asked.

Looking over her shoulder, Olive said, "Not this. *That*. Our childhood adventures at Howler Hall."

Kestra looked back and caught my eye. "I think maybe we are in shock."

We fell into silence but as the brighter lights of the farm meeting point came into view, there was an increasing restlessness in the mouse pack on my hip. Looking up, I saw a whirl of bats crossing in front of a moon that now looked much smaller, despite casting plenty of light. I felt sandwiched between nearly inaudible squeaks and chirps from below and above. They wanted me to do something, I was sure of it. Percy jumped down from Jilly's arms and circled my legs, adding his mew to the chorus.

"What's going on?" Jilly asked.

"Nothing. I need Keats, that's all. You go ahead and I'll go with Percy to find him."

"Okay, but stay in touch."

I nodded. "Heading to the truck to get my phone. Can't stand being without it."

Jilly moved up alongside Olive, but Kestra fell back with me and said, "I'll come with you."

"You'll need to stick with Jilly. The cops will do a head count. But there is something you could do for me first." Beckoning, I forced my way through the cornstalks and into the maze. "Come on. It'll just take a sec."

"Seriously?" she grumbled, following me. "Why?"

"Kess, I need something."

"More than saving your life from a pig?" Her teeth glinted in a grin. "Joking. I'd give you the shirt off my back."

She was joking, but that's exactly what I needed.

CHAPTER TWENTY-THREE

I t wasn't fair to leave Kestra in the corn maze wearing a Wonder Woman costume two sizes too large, but sometimes the ends justified the means. I knew she was intrepid enough to figure something out, and I wanted to escape unnoticed.

Percy loped alongside me to the truck. Just two cool cats—one fluffy orange, the other in a puffy black costume too tight for comfort but considerably warmer than Wonder Woman's garb. Kestra had given me her mask, too, but I was carrying it now, along with Millicent's case. I did my best to support the mouse, but there was no question it was still a bumpy ride.

Keats was waiting for me when we got to the parking lot. Perhaps he followed the bats, too, because his blue eye kept drifting up to the swirl overhead.

I let everyone into the truck but the bats. "It's coming up to eleven," I said, pulling out of the parking lot with the lights off. "Halloween is nearly over, and I can't say I'm any fonder of it than I was a week ago. Now I don't even like candy apples. What's left?"

Keats put his paws on the dashboard and grumbled at me to get a move on.

"Yeah, I know. Asher will figure out where I've gone before long and I need to do this. Millicent wants to go home and deserves peace and quiet after all she's been through. That was far too boisterous for a mouse. It was a bit much even for me."

The dog mumbled something unflattering that made me growl back. "I am not old. Or soft. Back-to-back adventures do take a toll sometimes. I'm not a born athlete like Asher, you know."

Oh, he knew. But I was doing pretty well for a former paper-pusher who flexed mind over muscle.

Percy rubbed against my arm and I thanked him, while still nudging him back into the passenger seat. He was a little too close to Millicent for her comfort or mine. It was innocent, no doubt, but it was always best to anticipate the worst.

And on that note, I gunned it, happy that I was learning Thistle-down's back routes. Thelma had given me a couple of grand tours in her Land Rover and while her driving had been as sedate as her roller set curls, something told me she could hit it hard when neces-sary. And what's more, that it *had* been necessary. When it came to my senior friends, it was always best to anticipate the best.

The drive was no more than 10 minutes and if all went well, I could be back before Asher came out of the maze. Jacob Wiebe was the bigger threat, having been assigned to keep an eye on me. He wouldn't hesitate to rat me out and curry favor with his superiors.

At the next red light, I texted Cori and asked her to distract the young officer. It would be her pleasure, I knew, and she accepted that I was on "mouse detail" without further question.

Waiting for the light to turn, I told the pets, "I'm going to take Millicent into the attic where the bats can keep an eye on her. They're obviously friends."

Finally, we passed the schoolhouse library and I made the last left too fast. The mouse's squeak took on a grating note that felt like a rebuke. "Sorry, Millicent. I forget Keats and Percy know when to dig in. You should see the upholstery in here. But for your sake, I hope you never do."

I decided to leave the truck one street over from the house. If I remembered correctly, there was a parkette that separated the two quiet roads and I could run across easily enough. The main route would be safer but could also attract attention. I wasn't the only one out in costume, but no one else would be accompanied by a cat and dog. The mouse wouldn't be visible and hopefully the bats had gone ahead to serve as homecoming committee.

"Boys, I'm going to need to examine the attic and make sure nothing of Eliza's was left behind by the thieves. Keats, you can sit this one out if you want but it would probably go faster if you came up in your backpack."

The dog's next mumble was far from cheery and I teased him, "Maybe you're getting old and soft."

He didn't sass me back, which meant his cheer truly was dampened by the prospect. The combination of backpack and bats was asking a lot. But I doubted he'd say no. The only assignments he ever turned down involved water.

He gave a full body shake, as if to dispel the very thought.

"I feel like we owe it to Eliza to collect anything she hid in the house. I'm sorry she never came back to reclaim her things. They must have meant a lot to her once and it's such a violation that a precious gift was used to kill someone."

Pulling the truck into the shelter of bushes, I collected my go-kit from the rear and then followed the pets through the parkette. Olive had told me where the key was hidden and I was optimistic we could get through this mission quickly and without mishap. With Keats and Percy on the job, we'd locate anything that was meant to be found. And with Paige Ogilvy in custody, there was no reason to worry about anything worse happening. This chapter in Thistle-down's life would soon be over. How the story ended for Olive remained to be seen. She had proven more resilient than I expected, but now the agent that sold her this blighted gem had thrown another log on the fire that was sending "home sweet home" up in smoke.

The three other houses on the street were already shut down for the night, leaving two streetlights to do the heavy lifting. I knew my way around well enough by now and had both a flashlight and my phone. The key was where Olive had left it and we headed inside and directly upstairs.

"No distractions," I said, although my heart stuttered briefly when the beam of my light hit the face of the creepy doll on the window ledge. "Hey, Beauty. *Not*. Olive should have auctioned you off to the rabid collectors of old stuff. Maybe the Langman sisters will take you back."

In the front bedroom, I dropped my kit and pulled out Keats' backpack. For once he didn't play dead, which I appreciated as that always made the job of strapping him in even harder. Maybe the solution was asking permission first.

Probably not. Nothing that felt like restraint was ever going to fly with this dog. But sometimes we did need to lift off.

Slipping the straps over my shoulders, I hoisted the dog and walked into the closet. I unhooked the ladder and maneuvered it into place. It fit nicely in a couple of grooves in the frame of the trapdoor, which was still open.

"Percy, want a lift?"

He meowed a negative and scaled the ladder with more ease than I could, especially with a forty-pound dog on my back and a mouse riding at my side.

"Almost home, Millicent. If you have any pull with your bat friends, could you ask them to stay gone till we're done?"

She chittered away in what sounded like a cheerful monologue. It seemed she was happier to be home than Olive would be.

It was a large attic with all the spookiness I expected. There was nothing in the single room that ran the length of the house but dust, cobwebs and the piles of acorns that had kept Millicent going while chained to the locket. Someone had cleaned the place up a little because there wasn't much evidence of critters.

"I guess the bats are out doing bat things on the biggest bat night of the year," I said. climbing over the last rung. I knelt on the floor and released the mouse, while holding Percy by the collar Millicent shot across to a wall and climbed up to perch on a crossbeam. When she was safe, I released Keats from his backpack.

Finally, I got to my feet. At my height, the only place I could stand straight without banging my head was in the middle of the room.

I walked from one end of the house to the other, shining my light around and looking for loose boards, and other signs of nooks and crannies. Meanwhile, the cat and dog fanned out, sniffing. It was only a few minutes before Keats went into a point near the back of the house.

Millicent was there ahead of him. She sat on a beam over my head firing off loud, repetitive cheeps like an automatic rifle.

"Got it, got it," I said. "Leave me some hearing for the next job, okay?"

Percy looked up to make sure I had his attention and then made one of his classic sweeps over a space on the floor. There was enough dust that I could see his paw and claw prints.

I could also see other footprints that didn't look big enough to belong to the two male police officers.

"Someone was up here looking for more treasure, too. Percy, I'm going to guess from your enthusiasm that she didn't find it?"

He threw his other paw into action for the combined sweep. If we were outside in soft soil or gravel, I would almost think... No. Surely not. There couldn't possibly be room for a body in the floorboards.

If there were, I would want to head back down that ladder pronto. Some things I was happy to leave to the folks who'd survived cop college. Old bones, for example. I was reasonably sure it was nothing of more recent vintage, or it would have been found far sooner. We'd had a hot summer and warm fall.

I knelt again and dragged my go-kit to the spot Percy had marked up pretty thoroughly. "Boys, tell me honestly. Should we call in the professionals?"

Percy started sweeping again, his claws raking the floorboards. Keats mumbled a command that sounded urgent and Millicent fired off another round of cheep ammo.

"Fine. But if I'm traumatized for life, find yourself a new sleuth. Just step over my weary body and carry on."

Keats added his paws to the flurry and so much dust flew up that I sneezed.

"Stop already. I'm on it."

Reaching into my go-kit, I found a utility knife and silently thanked Edna again. She was so right about being prepared. A bunker might not be a bad idea after all. Somewhere out near the new orchard, where the Macintosh apples were bigger and better.

Keats poked my cheek with his damp nose and I blinked a few times. For a second, I'd spaced out. I must be more exhausted than I realized. I hadn't slept last night but I used to be able to power through a few days at a stretch without missing a beat. Maybe I *was* getting old and soft.

This time the dog nipped my forearm. Not hard. Just enough to ground me in the present, where teeth were sharp and knives sharper.

As if to underscore his point, a bat swooped into the attic and fluttered around my head. I ducked and it circled once before disappearing through what looked like a small crack in a low corner at the side of the house. Somehow this gap had eluded exterminators and given the bats a free pass to come and go as they liked. It didn't look like they spent a lot of time here.

Taking a deep breath, I ran the knife around the board that riled Percy most and found a place I could dig in. The board came up easily and underneath was a vast cubbyhole that most certainly could have held a body, if properly arranged.

To my unending gratitude, the only thing in that hole was a burlap sack bearing the name Pyle Enterprises.

"Alonzo Pyle," I said. "This must have come from him, or at least their family store."

I leaned down and pulled out the sack. Then I replaced the floorboard and backed away, with both pets following closely. Millicent also followed on a beam, continuing her rat-a-tat cheeping.

In the end I was glad I had moved, because when I shone the flashlight inside the sack, what I saw made me jump onto my knees. In the corner, I would have hit my head on the roof.

There was nothing overtly horrifying about a heavy silver candlestick holder.

But the generous amount of a dark substance around its sharp edges suggested this was very likely what broke the skulls of the pumpkin patch residents.

"The murder weapon," I said. "Let's go."

CHAPTER TWENTY-FOUR

I didn't remember much of my hasty descent from attic to bedroom to main floor. It wasn't until I stepped into the front hall that my brain reconnected. The "on" switch was Keats going into a point. He had turned in the direction of the dining room, and Percy, who basically skidded down the banister, took a leap that way.

Although the front door was straight ahead, I had no choice but to follow my cat. By this time he was out of sight, so I couldn't assess his hackles. Keats, unfortunately, had gone straight to a five-alarm fire. We were in trouble, and Percy was headed right into the flames.

There was no point in hiding my presence. If someone was in the house, they would have heard us clomping around upstairs. No doubt I'd had a rather animated conversation with my animal friends. I had definitely bid Millicent a sad goodbye, but she had run off as if we'd never been close at all.

Now there was someone lurking in the dining room, perhaps waiting to go up after I left and hoping to find a more valuable treasure. Well, the candle holder would be a treasure for the police, especially as they could close two open cases in one fell swoop. But the piece wasn't likely high quality and would never have brought in the big bucks at auction.

Or maybe it would, given the recent interest in true crime. That's probably what had driven the price of Eliza Ormiston's belongings so high. The Langmans were hoping to cash in on the ghastly pumpkin patch discovery, not knowing the victims' identities.

I might still have time to get out without an altercation if Percy would just join me of his own volition.

Standing where I was, I called his name. And then again, louder. No response.

Finally I resigned myself to meeting a fellow intruder.

All I could do was prepare.

I groped for my phone in the convenient front pouch in the cat costume and pressed Jilly's number. Then I heaved the go-kit over my left shoulder and tucked the candlestick in its burlap sack under the same arm. That left my right hand free for the flashlight.

I was as prepared as I could be.

The problem, I discovered as I walked into the dining room, was that one could never fully prepare for an encounter with a gorilla.

That's what was standing in my flashlight's beam.

Not a real gorilla, of course, but a costume that looked remarkably lifelike. With a lot more padding, it could probably pass in more diffuse lighting. With my high-powered flashlight, it was very clearly a fake. What's more, it smelled of mothballs.

That was what gave the intruder away.

I recognized that costume from my digital trip through the newspaper archives with Thelma and Millicent. This was an heirloom of a different sort, embraced by a family who enjoyed both prominence and costume parties.

Prominence was the issue tonight, I knew. There was a very good chance the furry fabric—or was it real fur?—concealed a different sort of family gorilla. The type that would protect legacy at all cost. The type that would kill and leave someone else holding the bun prong if it meant keeping a clean reputation in the community they'd helped establish. The type that would worry about the younger gorillas coming up behind in the Thistledown rainforest.

"Hi there," I said, making sure I projected clearly for Jilly on the other end of the phone. After her first hello, my friend had fallen silent, waiting for clues. "I'm surprised to see you here at Olive's house. You really leveled up your costume."

I hit the lights at my end of the large dining room. All was as I remembered. The furniture was sparse. A table and chairs sat against one wall and a sideboard against another. That was about it, aside from the antique platter on the plate rail.

The gorilla said nothing, but one floppy paw came up and hit the light switch at the other end of the dining room, leaving us in darkness again.

We repeated the move twice before I gave up.

"Fine, have it your way," I said. "My flashlight is good for a bit. But if I had a family heirloom like your costume, I'd want to show it off. Mind you, I'd probably air it out, first. Mothballs are toxic."

I wanted to reveal the person's identity to Jilly, but if I pushed too hard too fast, I could end up in a brawl before anyone reached me to help. There was a double plot available in the garden suite for me.

"Look, I've never liked Halloween," I said, glancing around for Percy. "If you're going to bury me out back, could you skip the pumpkins and go with something summery? Not sunflowers. Maybe dahlias, like my mother. That's it! All my sisters are named after flowers. I'll take daisies, irises, violets and poppies, please. An ash tree in the back and ivy growing along the fence. Mom never envisioned it that way but we could have a Galloway memorial garden. What do you say?"

The gorilla said nothing. If it was aware of the cat on the sideboard, it didn't let on. However, the costume head wobbled this way and that, probably trying to get a fix on the dog. The eyeholes were not well located. After all, it was decades old and designed before the fascination with Halloween took hold.

Keats was pacing in front of me, belly low, ready to bring in his first big game. A real gorilla wouldn't need to fret about a dog, even a heroic one. This moth-challenged relic was right to worry. That costume offered some protection, especially from an ear grab and an 18-claw scalp massage, but not enough to avoid a few good punctures. Something told me this suit was part of the valuable legacy to be protected.

"I'm not sure why you changed," I said. "Did you want to scare kids in the street? I don't think you were home from the auction in time to take your grandkids trick-or-treating."

"Shut. Up."

Ah-ha. I'd meant it as a glancing blow, but she'd taken it as a hard hit to the legacy.

"I'm just saying I liked you better as a witch. You and Paige and Blenda could have stirred up a nasty caldron of trouble." I flicked the lights and eased back into the doorway. "Oh wait, you did."

The lights went out again.

"You could have just walked right out that front door. I would have let you go."

"You wouldn't though," I said. "You had eyes on me. Or at least, that creepy doll did. There's a camera hidden inside."

A gorilla would never giggle, but Glennis Redding did. "I followed you from the hobby farm. Thought I'd better make sure you didn't do anything stupid."

I nodded, and then realized she probably couldn't make out subtle gestures or movements through those eyeholes. The costume was meant for a man. Specifically, her grandfather. And she'd been filling his costume for many decades. "I was worried about the mouse, you see. Millicent. She'd been dragging around Eliza Ormiston's locket for a while. That's what got the Sprockets all worked up.

And then Olive. You must have missed it when you cleared out Eliza's belongings from the attic."

"That was Paige," she said. "I have no interest in hocking heirlooms. She's the one who's broke."

"You seemed quite engaged in the bidding war tonight. You got some nice pieces, Glennis."

Gorilla shoulders went up and down. "I agreed to generate interest, that's all. As a team player. We knew Heddy Langman wouldn't let the best things go."

"Plus, I'm sure you wanted this place thoroughly cleared out while you still had access. Too bad Olive didn't change the locks." I shone the light in her eyes. "Did we get all the bodies your grandfather buried?"

This time the light came on by her own paw.

"You take that back, Ivy Galloway. My grandfather was a pillar of the community."

"More like a killer of the community," I said. "But okay."

She took a few clumsy steps forward. With several decades on me and a bulky suit, she shouldn't win this fight. But it was always risky with people in the grip of insanity. It was hard to get a good look at her eyes but I thought I detected the familiar glazed look of the psychopath.

And if there was one lesson I'd learned, it was that you never get cocky with psychopaths. More unpredictable than a whole ark full of rescue animals. For all I knew, she could have a gun hidden in that costume. If she did, I wanted to know it, so I'd need to goad her a little more. Not too much. Just enough to decide if my pets were in peril.

"Hey," I said, walking around the room now. "Did your granddad always dress up in that suit when he offed people? Was it a Halloween ritual?"

"My grandfather killed no one. At worst, he hid a few bodies for other people." She gestured at the burlap sack. "Like the Pyles, perhaps."

"Hiding bodies is still a crime. But we'll let the police figure it out. Hopefully what I'm carrying will give them something to go on."

The gorilla head moved up and down, scanning me. "You got nothing."

"Pretty sure I've got a murder weapon. My pets agree, and you saw for yourself how effective they are in such matters."

She walked along the wall till she was blocking the doorway into the front hall. I didn't particularly want to leave the house by the kitchen door. It was too close to the excavated garden for comfort and I might lose my footing. Or a pet.

"Prove it," she said. "And I mean it. Because I'm armed, Ivy. My father insisted I learn how to use a gun. I never knew why until he brought me into the family business."

Okay, so she had a gun. It wasn't visible, so it must be inside the gorilla suit. It would take some time to doff the furry gloves and fish it out. On top of that, she'd need to show some agility to take aim and fire. I didn't think her execution of my execution would be easy. However, errant bullets could do as much damage as those fired well.

"Did you know what you were inheriting when you stepped into their shoes?" I asked. I wanted to make more paw puns but Keats' blue eye told me to scale it back a bit. He must have sensed she was getting to the boiling point. We didn't want that kettle to whistle before the police arrived.

And, with my gift—or curse—of empathy, I could understand what a weight this had been on Glennis all her adult life. How must she have felt when she learned she wasn't just getting a family business, but a family secret? How many other bodies were buried in homes her grandfather sold?

The gorilla head moved from side to side. Well, it mostly stayed where it was but I could tell her head moved inside. It was a loose fit. "I was barely twenty when Dad pulled me aside and explained why our business was so successful in a small community. It had never struck me that there weren't all that many houses to sell. Yet we always had more money than we needed."

"Wow. That must have come as a shock."

The head moved up and down. "I had no idea."

"If you don't mind my asking... were you forced to participate in the family side hustle?"

Another feeble shake. Then she lifted the collar to take a deep breath. Underneath, her face was still green from the witch makeup. "By the time I took over, it was just maintenance mode. Keeping a lid on what had already transpired. Houses don't change hands that often around here and major renovation isn't common, either. It was easy enough to take care of transitions." She dropped the collar and then lifted it again. "The worst part was that I didn't know everything. Even Dad didn't know everything. Grandfather got very... well, creative."

I tried to suppress a shudder and succeeded admirably. "You mean bodies could pop up anywhere at any time? Like they did here?"

"It happened. I had a record of all his transactions but sometimes he did private sales. There were surprises. I had to be alert and prepared. It was tiring."

"I can imagine." And I really could. Since she was 20, Glennis had been expecting bones to turn up like Easter eggs. I very much wanted to know how she remedied those situations, but it was better left to police. Besides, there was something more pressing I wanted to ask. "Glennis, I'll show you what I found in the attic if you'll tell me why you killed Blenda Mushing."

She dropped her collar again and her furry black fingers fluttered. "That wasn't in the plan. None of this was in the plan."

"I know." My voice found an even gentler note. "You just wanted to protect your legacy. For your father and grandfather."

"And my kids and grandkids."

"But Blenda stuck her nose in," I prompted. "Or did it start with Paige? Wait, I bet Paige found that foot before we did."

The gorilla head swiveled and she grunted, "Humerus."

"Humorous? It doesn't sound that funny to me." I mean, it sort of did, but it wasn't the right time to laugh.

"*A* humerus." She yelled "a" through the costume, and then tapped her upper arm for good measure. "Paige found one at the Hull house when she was doing completely unnecessary landscaping. Dug around the old shed and up popped an arm bone."

"Which she then used for leverage," I suggested. "It was clear to anyone that she wanted your job. Your life. She even dressed like you."

"Exactly! She went to my stylist and got my exact color and cut. Can you believe it?"

"Oh, I can. I spotted her ambition the first day we met. Thelma Tilrow says it's hard to get a foothold in any business in this area—particularly if there is a legacy, such as your family's. I'm going to guess you tried to buy Paige off. Told her you'd retire and hand over your client base. I heard you talking to your husband at the legion hall tonight about closing up shop."

Slumping for the first time, Glennis began sliding along the wall again. Her posture told me she loved her husband. Loved her kids. This was going to be hard on them all. In hindsight, all she had to do back in the day was step out of the gorilla suit but it probably felt like her own skin. A thick, furry hide that kept her from experiencing life to the fullest. All families brought legacies, but some were harder to carry around than others.

"It was all going to be fine," Glennis said. "Paige and I came to an understanding. But by then Blenda was involved. Paige brought her in to do some so-called energy work"—she shaped her furry fingers into quotation marks—"to give the Hulls peace of mind. After that, Blenda was popular for the first time. Her sage and spells and peacock feathers became all the rage. Paige backed her. She didn't realize Blenda was so—"

"Greedy?" I suggested. "Not to mention a fraud. She was bilking people and hurting her peacock. I doubt many will be sorry to see her go."

The paws went up and out in an "am I right?" gesture. "But still, I didn't want that to happen. I only wanted to scare Blenda. She had suspicions, you see. Started poking around. Asking too many questions."

"Sounds like Blenda," I said. "So you invited her to the maze. For a meeting of witches."

"She invited me. I think she was going for some sort of witch ritual vibe. I set the pig loose before going in. Thought it would shake things up and keep you clowns busy."

"And then what happened?" I pressed.

"When I joined them in the center of the labyrinth, Blenda didn't like what I had to say. She started shoving me, so I grabbed that prong thing out of Paige's purse. She'd held it back at the auction." There was a long pause. "Maybe she was going to kill Blenda herself. Or me. Or both." She flung up her paws. "That's why I worked alone all these years. You can't trust people."

"But you got to the prong first," I prompted.

"Yeah. I was only trying to show Blenda I meant business but she lost her balance and I guess I lost mine." The paw went to her chest. "I don't think Paige even realized what happened. She just stood there, so I ran. I could hear your crew coming. The noise and the fog helped, and I've run that maze for decades."

"Glennis, that will all be recorded. I saw security cameras in the maze. The police will know it was an accident."

I thought it was the right thing to say, but it was a fatal error. A failure of empathy. One look at Keats told me so.

There was a shift in the atmosphere that made the hair stand up along his spine and mine. Percy's fluff had never settled. He was so puffy it looked like a heavy wind could blow him away.

I tilted my head to the door. No sirens. Not yet. Where were they? Maybe I'd disconnected Jilly before she got the details.

It looked like I was on my own.

Well, I was never on my own. I had Keats and Percy, and there was always something more. There was no way we could accomplish all we did without a little extra help from somewhere.

But Glennis would have extra help from somewhere, too. She was driven by an unseen force to defend her family. She would fight like a real gorilla.

In that moment, I felt like I just couldn't do it. Not again. I was beat. Would adrenaline come to my aid as it always did?

Keats' mumble assured me it would. He was ready. Percy was ready.

What choice did I have, anyway?

I looked up at the big clock on the wall shared with the kitchen. It was six minutes till Halloween officially ended.

Time to get the party started.

CHAPTER TWENTY-FIVE

G lennis made the first move.

More specifically, she pulled off one fuzzy glove and reached into a front pocket, no doubt for the gun she'd mentioned. The other paw came up to remove the head of the costume. It looked like we'd be fending off a curious enemy, with a furred body and a green face.

Keats and Percy were crouched and waiting for my signal. I raised my hand, pulled in a deep breath and—

Someone jumped the gun. Perhaps quite literally.

It was the smallest among us who made the bold move.

Both Keats and Percy looked up—way up—to track Millicent running across the plate rail. I didn't know how she got there but she was clearly a mouse on a mission. I thought she might shoot down into Glennis's collar to give her a fright, but her plans were grander.

When the mouse reached the huge antique platter Glennis had presented to Olive as a housewarming gift, she slipped behind the plate and suddenly, it tipped.

It came down like the blade of a guillotine, slicing the head of the gorilla costume out of Glennis's hand.

The head flew across the room and struck me in the midriff

about the same time as the plate hit the floor. I expected the latter to shatter into a million pieces but the costume slowed it and cushioned the fall. The plate broke into mostly large pieces that looked ready to slice and dice. I could not send my pets into the fray, which left me on my own.

Only I wasn't.

Far from it.

In a true Halloween miracle, a cloud of bats swirled down the stairs and into the dining room.

Not six. More like sixty. At least so it appeared, as I backed hastily into a corner. The winged scout that visited the attic earlier had come back with all its friends. They filled the large room and created a vortex of energy.

Keats slipped under the sideboard, but Percy held his ground, fascinated by the aerial show.

The bats fluttered and flapped around the room, rising and falling in what seemed like a choreographed dance. Glennis was staring up at them in horror when the undulating black curtain fell over her head and shoulders like a drop cloth. I was worried she'd swing at them but she just covered her hair and dropped to the floor, furry knees crunching porcelain.

I stooped and reached inside the go-kit for the last thing I expected I'd ever need: a large piece of netting. Then I slid the burlap sack with the candlestick under the sideboard with Keats. He could guard it while I did the big game hunting.

Unfurling the first yard of netting, I waved it to clear the bats. They rose and swirled into the front hall. I took that moment to kick the gorilla head back across to Glennis. As it rolled up beside her, she grabbed it. In her moment of distraction, I lifted the net high and then flung it.

I snagged my first gorilla.

The bats came back in, circled the dining room once and then swarmed up the stairs to the attic.

As soon as they were gone, Glennis began thrashing under the net. There was so much fabric it would be hard for her to locate her gun, but she might be able to grab a shard of the platter and slice her way out of this bind.

I wasn't sure of my next move, but Keats had decided on his. He leapt up onto the sideboard beside Percy and they got ready to lunge.

"No," I yelled. "Stay."

I went a few steps closer, deciding on the best angle to tackle Glennis. My cat costume had good padding. All I had to do was keep my hands off the floor. I could sink them into the gorilla fur and pin her down until help arrived.

And that's exactly what I did.

Glennis put up a good fight, all things considered, but she had a lot of strikes against her. It was a good thing her family would never have footage of this undignified moment as part of their dubious legacy.

The grapple likely only lasted a couple of minutes until the front door hit the wall with a bang that made the broken china rattle on the floor.

"Dagnabit, Ivy, that is not how you trap a gorilla."

Edna's boots thumped and crunched, and then she grabbed me by the scruff and plucked me off my quarry.

Shoving me across the room to join my pets, she signaled Gertie and they moved in to show me exactly how to subdue a gorilla. By the time Officer Wiebe ran in a few minutes later, Glennis was both netted and bound, her costume head back in place.

I grabbed Keats, and Percy jumped onto my shoulder before Gertie marched us out.

"Ivy Galloway, you ruined a perfectly good piece of netting," Edna called after me. "Don't expect me to be so generous with my equipment after the end comes."

"Understood," I called back.

Asher met me on the porch with a baleful stare. "Well? What do you have to say for yourself?"

"I'll make my official statement later. For now, you'll find the murder weapon under the sideboard."

"The murder weapon?" His brow furrowed. "You already gave me the witch fork."

"Not that weapon. The other one. For the pumpkin patch people."

My brother looked away, lips pressed together. We teetered on the edge of inappropriate laughter over our terminology. Gertie must have felt it coming, because she whisked me to the stairs before it arrived.

When I was on the last stair, Jilly took Keats from my arms and dodged to evade Percy as he disembarked.

That left me free to fall into the waiting arms of my fiancé.

CHAPTER TWENTY-SIX

"I caught the whole thing," Kellan said, as he drove me to the schoolhouse library the next morning in my truck. "Glennis had one camera upstairs and another attached to the dining room clock. You looked right into the lens a few times."

"Watching Halloween go out with a flourish of bats," I said, trying to stop Keats from climbing into Kellan's uniformed lap. In another vehicle, Jilly was very likely trying to do the same with Percy and Asher. "Could you believe that swarm?"

"I could, actually. Growing up, we had a fair-sized colony in our utility shed. Mom insisted on letting them be. Kept the mosquitos in check, she said. Every evening at dusk, they'd fly out together in a cloud just like that one. And every evening, the neighbor's cat would come over to try to snag some. So, my mother assigned me as protector of the bats." He shrugged. "Is it any wonder I grew up without strong attachments to animals?"

I laughed. "Who knows, maybe this colony was returning the favor by protecting your fiancée and public safety."

"Yet it all started with a mouse." He turned into the library parking lot and found it full. "Should I pull rank and make someone move?"

"Nah. It's a beautiful day. Let's head down the street and walk."

He liked that idea enough to park much further away than necessary and we strolled back. It was warm but a brisk breeze sent red maple leaves floating down in spirals. They formed eddies along the curb, rustling and whispering. I stepped off the sidewalk and crunched through them, kicking some into the air. Keats jumped to snatch a few and then shook them rather savagely.

"What was that for?" Kellan asked, as the dog spit out a mangled mouthful.

"Frustration. He's still mad I didn't let him chew up Glennis's earlobe. Red maple leaves are a sad step down for a warrior."

Keats deliberately brushed against Kellan's leg and left bits of leaf. "What did I do? She's the one who called you off the gorilla."

"Maybe he wanted a photo op with big game. Think about it. That's a news story with legs."

Kellan slung an arm over my shoulders. "Sorry, Keats, I'm with Ivy on this one. I can't afford to have my best dog officer on leave with slashed paws. You got the glory in the maze. Isn't that enough?"

I shook my head. "Nope. Because Paige wasn't the true murderer and he knew that even without Wonder Woman's lasso of truth."

My fiancé waggled his eyebrows. "I liked that costume. Saw the farm's security feed. Can you keep it?"

"I had to keep it. It was so scratched up they wouldn't take it back."

"You don't say. Maybe I'll feel differently about Halloween from now on." He winked at me. "Or not. It's a night that puts fear into the heart of police officers in many parts of the world. Sanctioned buffoonery."

"What happened here only confirmed my ill opinion," I said. "I came out of it with a new respect for bats and mice, but I lost my fondness for pumpkins and candy apples."

"Pumpkins will rebound. They're unavoidable in farm country."

I slowed as we got closer to the library. Walks like these were few and far between for us and demanded to be savored. Besides, he would soon be caught up in finding the rest of the skeletons in Thistledown's gardens, attics and possibly foundations.

"Did you get a list from Glennis of where to look for the bodies?" I asked. Sometimes murder talk was a mood killer, but if the situation was well in hand, it was normally fine.

"Yeah. It wasn't an easy interrogation. She kept putting the gorilla head back on and Wiebe couldn't bring himself to take it away. Glennis's daughter used to babysit him, and he thought of them as family. So Asher had to step in and he did well. I'll need to keep him down here for a while."

"Not permanently, I hope?"

Kellan shook his head. "Can't afford to lose my best officer." He looked down at Keats. "Of the human variety. But we do need to build capacity here. When we get through the backlog we'll see where we stand."

"Do you know if Glennis's grandfather murdered any of these people by his own hand?"

He shook his head. "Unclear. I don't think she knows and she doesn't want to believe it. He certainly disposed of the bodies for Alonzo Pyle, Senior. Turns out there was plenty of evidence to put the latter away but someone must have tipped him off, because he left town just in time."

I stopped walking. "Do you think that's why Eliza and Alonzo Junior never came back?"

"Dunno. But when things slow down a bit, I'll see what I can find out."

"I know Vikki Tickle would appreciate that."

We went up the ramp to the library doors and there was very little room inside. Luckily we had an agile sheepdog to carve a path through the crowd to the back room, where Cori and Bridget stood behind a lectern on stage, with a covered dog crate beside them.

"Finally, Galloway. Rescue waits for no woman," Cori said, over a microphone that she really didn't need. Her voice had the piercing quality of Millicent the mouse. Kellan must have agreed because he covered one ear. It was a mistake because it only made Cori speak up. "On the stage, Ivy. For some reason, you're the fan favorite today. Well, Keats, anyway. Percy's already—" She lurched and swallowed the last word as the cat landed on her shoulder. He looked much bigger and brighter on the small, dark-haired woman.

I let Keats lead me to the stage and joined Cori and Bridget. The crowd applauded and Keats did a play bow that made Cori roll her eyes. It was nice to see him enjoying the moment. My dog liked to work and would never let fame go to his head. Even if he did, there was someone ready and willing to put him in his place. Several some-ones, actually. Maud Gentry was here with Frost, who snaked up to the stage and literally pushed Keats off. Annie had even more clout with him but the party scene wasn't for her and she stayed home.

"I'm not one for a long song and dance," Cori said, which was true. "So I'll cut to the chase and say we've decided to place only one dog today. We welcome the rest of you to try again next year. But the cards were stacked against nearly everyone this time." There were groans and complaints and Cori waited for people to subside before continuing. "Honestly, our panel of judges struggled to choose even one winner with all the hubbub. But in the end, we decided to trust Bailey, our shepherd mix, with..." She drummed gloved fingers on the lectern. "Nigel Byrd."

I probably wasn't the only one surprised by the outcome, but Bridget's dog, Beau, must have sensed depths in Nigel the rest of us couldn't know.

Everyone turned and then created a little space around the winner. Jilly nudged him forward, and said, "Go get her."

Nigel cleared his throat and then called, "I thank you for this honor. I would like to defer acceptance till your next competition and ask that you place Bailey with Olive Redding."

Olive turned to him, startled, and a flush rushed into her cheeks.

"Thank you so much, Nigel. But I've realized this isn't a good time for me to take on such a big responsibility. I'll be moving house again soon and the disruption isn't fair to a dog. So I also defer and forfeit to Vikki Tickle. I will happily support Vikki with the care of any and all pets."

It was easy to locate Vikki with her colorful shock of hair. "Oh, Olive, you know I can't handle that crazy kitten and a dog. As much as I'd love Bailey, I won't give up Goblin. So I hereby forfeit to your sister, Kestra Redding."

Cori's gloved fist pounded the lectern. "Are you kidding me, people? This isn't a democracy or a swap meet. No one gets to make decisions about our dogs but us. You are all hitherto banned from participating in our rescue events."

At least a dozen people shouted offers to take Bailey but Cori was resolute. In fact, I had never seen her so put out.

"I hate to say it but I actually feel for Cori," Kellan said. "Here she is bestowing a great gift and it gets passed around like a hot potato."

Keats must have felt for her, too, because he stuck with Cori while Frost went over to bring the Redding sisters together in a sheepdog knot. I hoped Kestra wasn't hurt that Olive had chosen Vikki Tickle over her. It was obvious that Vikki had the time, space and money for a dog. She had already seemed lonely and would no doubt grieve anew during discussions public and private about her long-lost sister.

"Everyone's so flustered about what happened," I said, frowning. "I bet if people had a few days to calm down, they'd be all over that dog. No one feels fully stable right now."

"I suppose. But a dog offers comfort and protection in times of turmoil." Kellan was still evaluating Nigel, his expression inscrutable. "Or so you always tell me."

"That was a romantic gesture, right? Nigel was trying to win points with Olive."

Kellan pursed his lips. "Not sure what that was, exactly."

"What else could it be? I told you he was interested."

He pulled me away to the fringes of the crowd. People were still milling about, disgruntled, and Cori left in a huff with Bridget, Beau and Bailey. Percy was still on Cori's shoulder and Keats ran by their side, but I knew my pets would turn back at the door.

"He's interested all right," Kellan said, "but maybe not in the way you think."

"Oh? Do tell."

Still checking for eavesdroppers, he said, "Ran Nigel's prints because he handled the murder weapon and found out he's a cop."

"A cop!" The words came out far too loud and I knew it.

Kellan rolled his eyes and refused to go on until the noise around us grew again. "Make that a former cop. He quit a good post in Boston about two months ago. Said he had PTSD."

"It's a lie?" I whispered now.

"Probably true. Most cops do, and he has good reason. Probably just wanted a fresh start. A do-over. Most cops never leave the force, even when they should."

"Like you running a hardware store," I said. "It's your secret dream."

He smiled at me. "Exactly. And what else did I say I was going to do if I ever surrendered my badge?"

"Farm chores? Flipping houses? Wait, wait... You're going to light a fire under my black label fertilizer." I grinned at him. "Not literally. It's combustible."

"Are you finished?" he asked. "Or maybe you don't really want to hear this."

I dropped the banter immediately and grabbed his hand. "Oh, I do. I guess I'm giddy with relief. And delight over being with my honey."

"Good answer. I'll fall for flirtation every time. Especially if—"

"No, I won't put on that Wonder Woman costume today, or any

day soon." I gave him a coy smile. "But you'll always know it's there... just waiting for a warm day to do some farm chores."

He was both intrigued and amused. "Let's give this another try, then." He surveyed the room once more with that casual cop glance I still hadn't mastered. "What was my potential backup career?"

I raised my hand. "I know, I know. Private investigator."

"Exactly. It's what a lot of cops do when they retire."

"Even when they retire at what... thirty-three? He can't be older than that."

"Good guess. And yet that is apparently what he's doing."

"Huh. Here in Thistledown? That seems odd."

He nodded. "I thought the same, so I made a few calls. What's more, I asked your brother to poke around."

"Oooh... and what did you find?"

Kellan leaned in and put his fingers to his lips. "He's investigating Olive."

"What?" It was too loud again and now he rested his finger against my lips.

"Probably Olive's former husband. Seems like the loser ex got away with a lot. Some are wondering if she knew more than she's letting on."

I shook my head, and my hand dropped to my side. Soft, warm ears arrived right on cue. "Jilly and I think Olive is solid. Perhaps more importantly... so does Keats."

"She probably just fell for the classic sociopathic charmer," he said. "And that's not a crime."

"Exactly. And hopefully now she can settle down in a new house and get ready for the right dog."

"Cori's not going to give her another chance."

Keats gave a saucy mumble and I interpreted. "There's more than one way to win a good dog."

"Yeah, harder ways."

I watched Olive and Kestra chatting, and noticed Frost was still sticking close to them. Frost was no fool. Had she assigned herself as security detail?

"What are you going to do about Nigel?" I asked.

"Same thing you're doing with the Redding sisters. Observing. If he's one of the good guys, he'll win something better than a dog."

"The girl?"

He pulled me away and I followed. "Not the girl, although romance isn't my field of expertise. What he'll win is a job. Policing is still his calling. He just needs a bridge back in."

"And you're the bridge?" I asked, squeezing his hand.

"Crime's the bridge. No cop with a record like his will be satisfied as a PI."

I stopped him and planted a kiss on his cheek. "I love the way your mind works."

He looked almost as happy as he had at the prospect of seeing Wonder Woman wrangling sheep.

Keats led us to the front door, white tip of his tail swaying. As we passed Thelma's checkout desk, Percy left the index cards he was rearranging and leapt onto Kellan's shoulder.

Our perfect little family headed outside and into the bright fall sunshine and I practically skipped as we headed back toward the truck.

"What's got you so happy?" Kellan asked.

"It's the day after Halloween." I raised his arm and did a twirl underneath it. "The most wonderful time of the year."

CHAPTER TWENTY-SEVEN

A week later, we all came back to Thistledown to help Olive move from the Ormiston house. She hadn't unpacked much, and there were plenty of people to help.

Asher and Kellan did most of the heavy lifting, alongside Jacob Wiebe and Nigel Byrd. Wendel Barrick and Rickie Merriweather were lending a hand as well. And naturally, Edna barked orders like a drill sergeant that went mostly ignored by the men. Kestra, Louisa and Zoe carried out boxes that Gertie packed with precision into vehicles. Even Thelma had turned the closed sign on the library to join the project, although she stood well out of the way with Maud Gentry.

Olive came down the front steps to join Jilly and me. We had done a token amount of work before deciding to kick back a little and enjoy the company.

"I can't believe this," Olive said. "I moved in here not knowing a soul just weeks ago. Now, the place is swarming."

"With more than bats, hopefully." Jilly smiled and patted Olive's arm. "This is what's known as 'community.' I didn't really understand the word when I moved to Runaway Farm. In Boston, Ivy and I were basically an island."

"Surrounded by a lot of people who weren't our tribe," I added. "No slight against cities, but we're small town all the way, now."

"Call me a convert," Olive said. "No one has ever stepped up for me like this before. Especially this lady, right here."

She gestured to Vikki Tickle, who was pulling up to the curb in the van she'd once painted with colorful balloons. Wendel had got it running again. Now, he came over to help her down from the driver's seat and I was happy to see they were becoming friends. Both had been lonely since their spouses died, and I'd seen the change in Wendel since he'd connected with Maud, Thelma and the Merriweathers. At first it was grudging but not anymore.

Vikki was in another vibrant outfit that spanned the color spectrum and her hair had fresh maroon highlights. "Plenty of room in the van for boxes," she called out. "It's all coming to my place, one way or another."

She had offered Olive the use of the cottage on her property until she was able to find a new agent and buyer for the land on which we stood now. At first, Olive had resisted. She didn't want to impose. It wasn't Vikki's fault the Ormiston home had been desecrated, or her responsibility to help Olive get back on her feet. But Jilly and I helped Olive to understand how it could be a win-win. Vikki wasn't the type of woman to offer unless she wanted to help. She saw something in Olive that went beyond a shared love of black cats. I wouldn't be at all surprised to find them roaring around in that van together, lifting spirits like helium balloons.

Vikki reached out to Olive now for a hug but the younger woman backed away. "Not into PDAs?" the senior said, not in the least offended.

"Oh, she is," Kestra said, coming over. "She's on the huggy side of the family. What gives, Olli?"

I raised my hand. "I know! I know!"

"It's nothing," Olive said, squirming a little. "I'm just stiff from packing boxes this morning."

"Big fat lie," Kess said. "You swanned around the house while I packed."

Olive glared at her sister. "I was in the attic sealing up a few gaps. The bats have already moved on, but I want to make sure the next owners have a better homecoming."

Waving my hand harder, I repeated, "I know why!"

Jilly laughed. "You might as well call on Ivy. She was that kid in every class and that exec in every boardroom."

"The know-it-all?" Thelma asked. "Me, too."

The librarian was another of my quirky kindred spirits. "But you're not going to like this answer. Olive is packing a mouse."

"Millicent?" Jilly asked. "Of course. That's why she's wriggling so much."

Olive's face flushed. "It's a strange sensation. She shot up my sleeve in the attic and refused to leave. I didn't have the heart to shake her out."

"She wants to go with you." I turned to Vikki. "Are you open to taking on another lodger?"

The hand she fluttered had nail polish in 10 shades. "Sure. The more the merrier. I worry about the cats, but I'm sure the girls will work it out."

I had wondered about Kestra's plans but didn't want to ask. Thistledown hadn't been her dream destination and I expected she'd roll on eventually. She had a bristling energy that required more stimulation. This town was a place to slow down and recalibrate, which was what Olive needed after the dramatic end of her marriage. Kess needed something else.

"I really can't thank you enough, Vikki," Olive said. "It was already an imposition without adding a mouse."

The old woman shrugged. "I'd like to say I draw the line at bats, but really, I can warm up to almost any animal."

"Maybe they'll turn up next Halloween," I said. "Although it would be hard to top this one."

Thelma directed a stern pucker my way. "Let's not try. We have enough challenges in hill country without local gorilla problems."

"I thought this was awesome," Kestra said. "An authentically terrifying Halloween. I'll be back every year."

"You're not staying?" Thelma asked. The slight slackening of her pucker told me she was relieved. Like me, she probably sensed that where Kestra went, trouble followed.

Kess tapped her phone. "Mom called earlier. Something's going on back home and she needs help."

Olive turned so quickly that the mouse literally dropped out of her sleeve. "Mom didn't call me."

Frost was at her feet in a flash and we all gasped as the dog picked up the mouse. We needn't have worried. The jaws that could be so savage with criminals were gentle when there was a tiny creature in need. She dropped the mouse in Olive's cupped hands as if it were a newborn puppy and the mouse jetted back up till her beady eyes were peeking over the coat's collar. The look Frost gave Olive was oddly sweet. These dogs didn't generally have a "sweet" setting.

I turned to Maud and her expression mirrored my own surprise. It wasn't about the mouse but the fact that Frost was often hanging around the new Thistledown resident. That didn't seem to have registered consciously with Olive, yet her fingers often dropped to Frost's head, just as mine did to Keats'. In fact, they landed there now, as Kestra walked over to calm her sister.

"It's about Gran," Kess said. "There was a situation at Howler Hall."

"What kind of situation? Is everything okay?"

"Olli, don't worry. You've got enough on your plate here. I'll head down and let you know what I find out." She unzipped her jacket and showed us a rust-colored sweater with a garish turkey on it. "Good thing I planned ahead. Thanksgiving is up next."

After making Kess promise to call as soon as possible, Olive let her new community closed in around her. I offered to give Kestra a ride to Howler Hall. It was less than an hour's drive and I wanted to see it again. Kess could give me the insiders' tour.

"No worries," she said. "Booked a seat on the bus and I can walk to the depot from here. I'd rather today be about Olli. She needs this."

"You need support, too," I said, following as she eased away from the crowd. I was impressed at how far her relationship with Olive had come in such a short time. When I got home, I was going to put my warring goat siblings to work, too. A joint project might well heal the rift.

"I'll be fine." She beamed at me. "I think my dream dog is waiting just around the corner."

I looked at Keats, who was trotting between us and panting happily. "You know what? I think so, too."

We walked Kestra to the main road and she sprung a hug on me. "You've given me a lot to think about, Ivy. Thank you."

"My pleasure. Just be careful, okay?"

She backed away and grinned at me. "I'm always careful."

I laughed. "I always say that. And it's never true."

When she was gone, I went back and beckoned for Maud to join me. "What's with Frost?" I whispered. "She's not usually that friendly with newcomers. She hasn't pranked Keats all morning."

Maud stared at the beautiful brown-and-white border collie standing beside Vikki Tickle's van with a small crowd. "I think she has a crush on Olive."

"Our dogs don't get crushes. Do they?" My fingers reached for Keats. "Not serious crushes. Keats is fond of Cori, though."

Still observing, Maud frowned. "I've been worried about Frost. Since Annie came home and the pups weaned, I think she's felt at loose ends. I give them equal time but it isn't enough. Annie is the first dog of my heart, and I bred this line for intense connection."

"You wouldn't let Frost go, would you?" There was a note of alarm in my voice that made Keats nudge my hand. "She's your dog."

Maud found a smile as she glanced down at Keats. "He's my dog, too. But I let him choose where he wanted to go. If Frost chooses someone else, I have to honor that."

"Well, maybe she won't. Olive isn't that special. Is she?"

"All in the eye of the beholder, I guess." Her smile grew stronger. "I probably wouldn't have said you were that special if I'd seen you leave your corporate office that day. But you turned out to be worthy of this dog."

I knelt and hugged Keats. "Maybe Frost should come to the farm for a bit. See if she gets over the crush."

Maud nodded toward the house, now nearly empty. "Look what happened with Eliza and Alonzo. I'd rather endorse a union than have my dogs elope. They might not always end up with the right people. This way, I can vet someone thoroughly." Her eyes narrowed. "My process is more stringent than the Mafia's. I put my heart into this lineage for decades and I don't need fancy gloves to back me up."

"We'll back you up, too," I said. "Always."

Kellan came over, helped me to my feet and pulled me close. "We're ready to ship out and start over at the other end."

I grinned at him. "I have good news. The mouse is moving, too."

My fiancé's face fell. He was no doubt imagining a life where spontaneous hugs were impossible, due to the risk of crushing a tiny passenger. To his credit, he swallowed hard and smiled. "She's coming to the farm? Isn't that a bit risky?"

"Everything is risky for a mouse. There are two cats at Vikki Tickle's but the mouse has chosen to go with Olive."

His relief was almost comical. "Good. I'm glad there's a happily-ever-after for Millicent. Call me a romantic."

"My romantic," I said, waving goodbye to Maud as Keats began herding us to the truck. "How did I get so lucky?"

Asher's truck was parked next to mine, and he was helping Jilly into the passenger seat. Percy was on his shoulder and I really don't think my brother noticed. He moved with his usual athletic grace as he came around to the driver's side and Percy rode the wave with equal ease.

Kellan watched them, too. Then he opened the door for me and I climbed in and welcomed Keats onto my lap. "How'd we get so weird?" he asked.

"Let me tell you about it," I said. "Once upon a time, on a Halloween long, long ago..." The door closed rather abruptly and cut me off. "His loss," I told Keats, laughing. "It's a really good story."

Ivy wants to skip her class reunion, but a tempest in the beekeeping community sends her back into the hive of stinging secrets and rivalries. Join the team on their next crime-solving adventure in *Bee All and End All*.

Interested in hearing more about my writing and my dogs? Join the Ellen Riggs newsletter at **ellenriggs.com/opt-in**.

RUNAWAY FARM & INN RECIPES

Fall Fair Chocolate Apple Cake

Ingredients

- 2 large eggs
- 1 1/2 cups white sugar
- 1/2 cup butter, melted and cooled
- 1 cup buttermilk
- 2 teaspoons vanilla extract
- 2 cups all-purpose flour
- 3/4 cup unsweetened cocoa powder
- 2 teaspoons baking powder
- 3/4 teaspoon baking soda
- 1/2 teaspoon salt
- 2 cups peeled, cored, and shredded apple (2-3 apples)
- 3/4 cup chocolate chips
- 1/2 cup walnuts (optional)

Instructions

1. In a large bowl, beat sugar and eggs until frothy. Then whisk in melted butter, buttermilk and vanilla extract.
2. In another bowl, stir flour, unsweetened cocoa powder, baking powder, baking soda, and salt until thoroughly mixed.
3. Add the dry ingredients to the wet ingredients, stirring till combined. Stir in the shredded apple, chocolate chips and nuts, if using.
4. Pour into a 9 x 13 x 2 inch baking pan lined with parchment.
5. Bake at 350 degrees for about 30 minutes or until a cake tester inserted into the center comes out clean.
6. Remove pan from oven and let cool on a wire rack.

More Books by Ellen Riggs

Bought-the-Farm Cozy Mystery Series

- A Dog with Two Tales (Prequel)
- Dogcatcher in the Rye
- Dark Side of the Moo
- A Streak of Bad Cluck
- Till the Cat Lady Sings
- Alpaca Lies
- Twas the Bite Before Christmas
- Swine and Punishment
- The Cat and the Riddle
- Don't Rock the Goat
- Swan with the Wind
- How to Get a Neigh with Murder
- Tweet Revende
- For Love Or Bunny
- Between a Squawk and a Hard Place
- Double Dog Dare
- Deerly Departed
- Think Outside the Fox
- Mouse of Ill Repute
- Bee All and End All
- Sheep with One Eye Open
- Roo the Day
- Till Death Zoo Us Part
- Hit the Road, Quack
- One Horse Open Slay
- Beg, Burrow or Steal

Bought-the-Farm Mysteries - Boxed Sets

- Bought the Farm Mysteries - Books 1-3
- Bought the Farm Mysteries - Books 4-6
- Bought the Farm Mysteries - Books 7-9
- Bought the Farm Mysteries - Books 1-10

Dog Town Series

- Ready or Not in Dog Town (The Beginning)
- Bitter and Sweet in Dog Town (Labor Day)
- A Match Made in Dog Town (Thanksgiving)
- Lost and Found in Dog Town (Christmas)
- Calm and Bright in Dog Town (Christmas)
- Tried and True in Dog Town (New Year's)
- Yours and Mine in Dog Town (Valentine's Day)
- Nine Lives in Dog Town (Easter)
- Great and Small in Dog Town (Memorial Day)
- Bold and Blue in Dog Town (Independence Day)
- Better or Worse in Dog Town (Labor Day)

Mystic Mutt Mysteries Paranormal Cozy

- I Want You to Haunt Me (Prequel)
- You Can't Always Get What You Haunt
- Any Way You Haunt It
- I Only Haunt to be with You
- All I Haunt Is You
- Do You Haunt to Know a Secret?
- All I Haunt for Christmas
- I Haunt You Back